LESBIAN STC
AND

# FF...

# TOP

# TO

# BOTTOM

EDITED BY
# HARPER BLISS

## Also from Ladylit Publishing

First: Sensual Lesbian Stories of New Beginnings
Summer Love: Stories of Lesbian Holiday Romance
Forbidden Fruit: Stories of Unwise Lesbian Desire

# CONTENTS

# INTRODUCTION

The first few erotica stories I wrote couldn't have been more vanilla. I kept writing and writing, until I noticed something unexpected. My characters started fighting for top, even began to tie each other up, and brought home paddles and floggers for their partners.

I'm by no means an expert on BDSM and transference of power, but I do know that, these days, I greatly enjoy a well-written story that is decidedly *not* vanilla.

As I've taken my own journey as a writer thus far, more and more BDSM scenes have crept into my stories until one day I asked myself: why not put out a call for submissions and gather a collection of stories I knew I would thoroughly enjoy?

This book is the result.

You don't need to be an expert on dominance, submission or anything else related to the BDSM sphere to be swept away by the supreme hotness of the tales in this anthology. They are kinky, daring and, at times, deliciously violent.

This book spans a broad theme and the stories vary greatly in subject matter and characters. There are teachers, naughty pupils, swimmers, runners, and quite a few professional Mistresses. There is tenderness and pain. Bruises and the softest of caresses. But above all, there's a great amount of pleasure to be found within the pages that follow.

Enjoy the pain.

Harper Bliss

# CHASING THE DRAGON
## S.E. HILL

I make the transaction over the phone, from the confines of my office. I need to see her again and I don't care about the cost. Like heroin… I need another hit. I adjust the buttons on my high-neck blouse, making sure they are secure before heading to my meeting. The lacy collar is tight. For an instant, flashes of her hand, squeezing the breath out of me while I orgasm, play in my head. Instinctively, I reach up to rub the side of my neck where the bruises from that night remain. As I walk out of my office, I hear the familiar ding of my phone, alerting me that I have a response to my request. I quickly glance at it as I walk towards the conference room. I am confirmed.

* * *

I am directing today's meeting. It isn't unusual for me to be in charge of most meetings I attend at KJB Enterprises, but this one is of particular importance because it is for the board. The pressure is high. I am proposing a complete restructuring of middle management. The cost-benefit analysis is irrefutable, in my opinion, and KJB is paying me quite well for my judgment. As a contracted barracuda, I am usually collectively reviled by the time my term is complete. I don't care about that much. I am compensated handsomely to cut the fat, and I am gone before things become really hostile. I like the variety. Each business presents a unique puzzle for me to solve. I enjoy zeroing in on each company's flaws and weaknesses, exposing them, and then destroying them one by one. Once that is done, all that is left is strength. It is a powerful feeling to give that to a company.

Perhaps that is why I need her so badly... because I am hoping that if I hire her enough times she will strip me bare until all I have left are my good parts. It isn't about giving up control. It is about freeing myself of my frailties and becoming empowered.

\* \* \*

The seduction starts almost immediately upon my confirmation. She lists what she requires from me over text. *Headphones.* Check. *Blindfold.* Check. *Rope.* Check. *Your complete trust.* I stare at that last statement. Do I trust anyone completely? I don't have time to think about it. As I click through my PowerPoint presentation, slide by slide, images of her requested tools keep interrupting my thoughts. I know, in theory, what she plans to do. After all, there is only so much one can do with those three instruments. Yet, my imagination is having a free-for-all. She owns my mind already, and she hasn't even laid a hand on my body. I glance at the clock, noting that it is only noon and I won't see her for ten more hours. How long our 'date' goes tonight depends on how much I can handle. That is always the deal. The cost is the same regardless of time. I can have her all night if I can endure it, although she informed me on our first introduction that no client ever lasted longer than three hours.

\* \* \*

The meeting went well. I receive handshakes and smiles from every board member as they head out of the door. I let out a deep breath and congratulate myself as the last one disappears around a corner, and I'm finally alone at the big oval table. I glance at all the now-empty seats and beyond, to the skyscrapers lined up outside the conference room windows, and lastly, at the clock again. Nine hours until my total release. I return to my office and try to concentrate.

\* \* \*

My phone pings again when I am wading through emails. I assume it's a text from her and feel slightly disappointed to discover it isn't. It is my friend Thomas, wanting to grab lunch. I accept his invitation. Thomas understands me, since we share an occupation… and the same predilections.

\* \* \*

"I'm meeting her again tonight." I share through bites of my salad. We are sitting outside at a little bistro, halfway between his office building and my own.

"Krista?" He raises his eyebrows, almost imperceptibly, but I notice. He is judging me. I can feel it.

"Yes," I reply. I focus intently on my salad, jabbing at the lettuce leaves with my fork.

"This is becoming more than a hooker-client relationship," he states matter-of-factly. His blue eyes stare at me, unblinking.

"No, it's not. I don't know anything about her!" I protest.

"But you want to. That's the problem." He wipes his mouth with his napkin and lays it on the table. He pushes his plate aside and throws some cash on the table. "I have to get back to work." He stands up from the table and starts walking away. Then he stops and turns around. "That's the thing though, Sarah… these kinds of relationships… you aren't allowed to know her. But she gets to know the very core of you. She knows what makes you tick, and manipulates it at will. That's the addiction of it. Be careful." Thomas walks away. I watch the back of his head as it disappears into a sea of people that crowd the sidewalk. Eight hours until I get to see her. Eight hours! Was I chasing the dragon, looking for a high that was never as good as the first one? I didn't think so. Every meeting with her was more intense; tested my limits; brought me closer to my own truth. The only dragon I am chasing is my own, I decide.

\* \* \*

Seven hours until I see her. I lean back in my desk chair and rub my temples. That is when she texts. *Feeling a little stressed today?* She is in my head... always in my head. *Why don't we do a warm-up exercise? You game?* I stare at my phone. I am game. I don't have to tell her that. She isn't really asking permission anyway.

She guides me through text, down my pants. She instructs me exactly how to touch my clit. She tells me when to get faster and when to slow down, how much pressure to use. I stare at my phone, and follow her instructions. She brings me to the brink of orgasm, and then suddenly tells me to stop. *You come when I let you*, she texts, *Remember that.* And then she is gone.

\* \* \*

Six hours. My cheeks are flushed and my panties are soaking wet. My clit is throbbing in protest at my sudden withdrawal of stimulation. I look up, breathless, realizing that I was so concentrated on her instructions that I forgot where I was. Anyone could have walked in and found me violating myself in my office. Yet, I didn't care. I'd do anything she asked. Anything. That was the challenge, wasn't it? To abide by her commands, even if they tested my boundaries and made me act in unfamiliar ways? I lean back in my desk chair and try to get my breathing under control. It's pointless to attempt any more work today. My mind is singularly focused. I decide to cut out early. I button my pants, grab my purse, and head to the gym. I need some kind of outlet for my sexual frustration, and a good workout seems like it will help, for now.

\* \* \*

I think about her while I run on the treadmill. Her dark hair... her intoxicating smell... her soft skin... her large breasts... the curve of her hips. I think about her tattoos... all of which I have memorized. But mostly, I think about her eyes and her hands. How they both punish or please me, depending on her mood. I think about what I actually know about her and realize my knowledge is scant. I know what she does for a living and practically nothing else. I want to know more. I want to know how she wakes up in the morning, how she spends her days off, what makes *her* tick. Maybe Thomas was right. Maybe I want more than I am entitled to within the boundaries of our current relationship. But maybe she wants more too? Is that wishful thinking?

I run for a full hour on the treadmill, my body drenched in sweat by the time I am done. My leg muscles are already sore and twitching with exhaustion the second I step off the machine. Yet, I still feel wound tight. I take a long shower, hoping the hot water will soothe the growing tension inside me. I know I'm fooling myself. I need her. I'm craving her. She is the only thing that can dull the ache. Krista. Four more hours...

\* \* \*

I eat a light dinner. I am not really hungry. I indulge myself with a glass of wine. She texts me as I take a long pull of my white, savoring the fruity sweetness.

*Thinking about me?*

*Always*, I answer.

*Good.* And she is gone again.

Two more agonizing hours left.

\* \* \*

She contacts me again at precisely nine o'clock, with instructions. I am to leave my front door unlocked. Her tools should be laid out on the console table directly next to the front door. I am to stand, naked, with my back to the door and wait for her arrival. I am not to look at her. I am not to speak to her. I obey.

\* \* \*

At exactly ten o'clock, I hear the click of my door opening. I smell her as she walks in, a combination of sex and vanilla and her natural scent that always instantly turns me on. I keep my back to her as requested. I can feel myself moistening already at just the smell of her, and the anticipation of what she is going to do to me.

I hear her grab something off the table. She walks directly behind me and slips the blindfold over my eyes and the headphones over my ears. She clicks the headphones on and my head is instantly flooded with some kind of tantric music I've never heard before. It pounds in my head, drowning out all ambient noise. I feel her grab my shoulders and direct me to the bedroom. When my knees hit the bed, she pushes me forward roughly, and then rolls me onto my back. She wraps the rope around my ankles and then trusses them up near my thighs, causing my legs to spread wide open for her and my back to arch. It is not painful, although I feel as if I'm in a constant, very deep stretch. I am fully exposed to her. I can't hide how glistening wet I already am. It embarrasses me that I am so obvious to her, so on display. I don't know what she is thinking when she looks at me. I can't see her or hear her. I can only feel her, continuing with the ties in a business-like fashion, circling my waist and then up around my wrists. She brings my arms over my head and ties them to the headboard, wrists bound together. I am locked in place, barely able to move. Then she gets another piece of rope and lays it taut across my neck. Where she has it secured, I have no idea. All I know is that if I try to raise my head up, I can feel it tighten against my throat, a further warning that my movement is limited. Then... nothing. Just as quickly as she ties me up, she is gone. Or, at least, I can't feel her heat near me. I wait, legs apart, tied down, blind and deaf.

Time slows down when you are exposed. I writhe uncertainly. Goosebumps prickle my skin every time I feel a breeze, thinking it might be her... hoping it was. I imagine she is watching me, surveying every inch of my flesh, judging whether it pleases her, thinking about how she is going to manipulate me at will. I get wetter still.

Then I feel it. Something cold. Ice? Water? It runs down my neck and the length of my torso. My muscles contract and I suck in my breath. Then, just as quickly as the sensation comes, it's gone. I am alone again. My mind is racing. The tension of the unknown starts mounting inside me, but so is excitement.

Then I feel her. The heat of her body is near my own. Is she hovering above me? Is she next to me? I can't place her, as hard as I try. I attempt to raise myself upwards, trying to feel her location. I want her soft skin against mine. The restraints quickly remind me that she lies just beyond my reach. I relax back into the bed. The warmth I sensed suddenly disappears. Or had it even been there in the first place?

Then, without warning, I feel ice against my hot, engorged clit. A quick touch, and then it is gone again. The only proof that it had even been there is the cold, melted water dripping from my clit down into my aching slit. Damn this blindfold! I am screaming in my mind with frustration, the music pounding, pounding in my head.

Then I feel an unfamiliar material lightly skimming my

body. Silk? I feel it caress my cheek and neck. It barely brushes against my breasts, making my nipples stiffen, and then travels down my body and through my legs. I feel my face being directed to the side by the lightest touch. Then the touch grows firmer. I can feel nothing but her hand running around to the back of my neck and then up into my hair, close to my scalp. She grabs a fistful of my curls and gently but firmly pulls back, making me expose the side and front of my neck to her. She is reminding me of my vulnerability. She is reminding me that I am hers. We are locked like that for a moment, tense. Then she feels me obey. My will is bent to however she wants to shape it and she knows it.

With this unspoken understanding between us, I feel her hand relax. It glides down my neck and continues, with purpose, down the length of my body. My clit is wet from the ice and I can feel how swollen it is. When she finally touches it with her fingers, I quiver all over.

She abruptly stops rubbing me almost as soon as she starts. Then, the silk scarf is back. She places it between my legs. I feel the top of it against my stomach, the other part I feel her push underneath me. And then she pulls both ends of the silk taut against me, from my clit all the way down to my ass. It is stretched tight between my lips, getting moistened immediately by my wetness. She pulls it, rhythmically, tight against me so it rubs against my clit and pushes against my threshold. She is fucking me with no penetration. I push my weight back against the silk, rubbing my clit against it, moans escaping my lips. I'm bucking as hard as I can against the restraints. I need her inside me. The music is thumping in my ears, but all I can hear are my own thoughts, silently begging her to enter me. Finally, I can't stand it anymore. "Please," I whisper. As soon as the word escapes my lips, I know it's a mistake. Her touch disappears. The now soaking wet silk vanishes. I try to raise my head again, and am immediately restrained by the rope. It is not my place to attempt to control how and when she touches me. My punishment is her lack of touch.

I try to sense her position in relation to me. I cannot. My clit is throbbing and my chest is heaving. I feel empty and like I need to be filled up by her. Minutes seem like hours. I am helpless. I begin to get angry. My obedience suddenly turns to hostility. How dare she leave me this way! Is she watching me? Is she letting my anger build? Watching my frustration grow with each passing second? I'm also mad at myself, for wanting her more and more as the minutes tick by, more than anything, ever.

And then suddenly I feel hot oil raining down on my entire body, making me gasp—a further punishment for my insubordination. The heat is intense, almost burning, and the scent of vanilla fills the room. I'm slick with the scented oil, and properly mollified. I need no more reminding that she is in control of everything that will happen to my body and that it is not my place to have anger. I'm prepared to acquiesce to whatever she wants. I am hers, all hers, for as long as I can stand it.

She rewards me for my renewed compliance with a gentle massage of my chest, thighs, stomach, and hips. I feel a tug and pull on my nipples, and then a piercing pain as she screws nipple clamps in place. Once they are secure, she pulls them ever so slightly. I suck in my breath and hold it. My breasts serve as a direct conduit to my groin and even though the feeling is extreme, the pain only serves to heighten my arousal. Her hands slip under my thighs and I suddenly feel her chin hit my stomach and run midline down my body. I feel her tongue for the first time and am reminded why I needed the wait and discipline. She knows my body better than me, and knew that I would get that much more pleasure if she made me wait for her attention.

She tastes every inch of me that her tongue can reach. No groove or crevice misses her consideration. Her tongue moves in every pattern imaginable, switching intensities in response to my body's cues. I tighten, about to orgasm, when I suddenly feel her hand grabbing my chin. She shakes my head side to side, screaming "No," without saying a word. I obey, trying with everything I have to dampen the urge to release. Her mouth is gone now, her hot breath just a memory as my own juices drip down my legs and dampen the sheets beneath me. I wait for her. I'm at the very threshold of coming and there is no turning back for me. I no longer mind being exposed to her. In fact, I'm enjoying that she can see how my body is responding to her every move. We are dancing, and I realize that I truly and completely trust her lead. It takes every ounce of self-control to wait, but I know that whatever she has in mind will be worth it and that I will be rewarded for my discipline.

And then it starts. Her fingers plunge into me without warning, fucking me insistently, without pause, over and over. I can feel her fingers exploring me from the inside as she fucks me. I can't even breathe, she feels so good. I scream with pleasure. It is all I wanted from the very start and she is finally giving it to me. I come all over her, my insides clenching and unclenching around her fingers. She stays inside me after I orgasm... just resting. She clicks off my headphones with her other hand and removes them. All I can hear is the sound of my own heartbeat in my ears and my breath coming in short gasps.

"Again," she says and begins fucking me some more. I can barely handle the sensation as she slides in and out of me. "*Again,*" she says louder as she increases her intensity. I can feel the tension building in my belly... and then I explode once more, this time longer, and more forcefully. The contractions are so strong that they almost feel like cramping. "Good girl," she whispers and gently pulls out of me. She removes the nipple clamps. The blindfold lifts and I finally get to lay eyes on her for the first time all night.

I just stare into her eyes, not really able to focus. I am exhausted and spent, limp and destroyed. I am wholly present and living right in the moment, all the stressors of my day erased.

"More?" she asks.

"No," I reply weakly, and then with more resolution, "No." She silently begins the work of untying me. I focus inward as she labors, quietly taking stock of my emotions. When she finally unties my legs, she helps me unbend them, massaging as she goes. Her touch feels loving now, and sweet, and the opposite of the commanding strokes she used on me just moments earlier.

"Can we… go out some time?" I ask her. It comes out of my mouth before I have time to think about it. "I know we don't know each other—" I start. She stops me.

"Correction. You don't know me. I don't know a lot of particulars about you… but I know *you*. You learn a lot about people in this business."

"Do you like what you know so far?" I am still naked, and feel as vulnerable as I could possibly be.

"Yes." She smiles. I had never seen her smile. It softens her. Makes her more human.

"How can I get to know you better?" I am leaning in close to her now, taking in her scent, feeling her heat. I want to curl into her lap like a puppy.

"Well…" She stares into my eyes. "You can take me out, wine and dine me, and we can have some perfunctory first date conversation. Or…"

"Yes?"

She holds up the rope and the blindfold. She gives a wicked grin. "Or… you can actually get to know *me*." She laughs. "And maybe, just maybe, you'll learn a thing or two about yourself in the process."

She instructs me on how to tie her to the bed, spread-eagled and naked. And then tells me to look in her tool kit. I open the duffle bag and my eyes widen. "I can use… anything in here?" I ask.

"Anything," she replies. No further instruction is

necessary. I place the blindfold over her eyes. I don't want her to see that she makes me nervous.

I purposely tie her sideways so that her head is in the middle of the bed. I want more of her tongue. I straddle her head and simply say, "Lick me until I say stop." She starts immediately upon my command. My eyes flutter closed as I sink into the warmth of her mouth. She will do this as long as I want, I realize. I let her. She kisses me until I come again. It takes every ounce of strength to tear my sex away from her tongue.

I stare at her naked body, taking my time because I know she can't see me doing it, pleased to see a hint of wetness dripping from between her legs. She liked doing that to me. Good. My confidence ups a notch.

I grab a riding crop from her bag and run it up and down her body. Then I set it down next to her. I will use it in a minute. I kneel down onto the bed and begin kissing and sucking her nipples. Her breasts are so large and soft and I get lost in them. I can't stop sucking even as I feel her breath quicken. I bring my hand down towards her clit, and when I find it, I quickly swat it with my hand, lightly, but hard enough to stun her. She gasps. I do it again. Then I rub her clit, exactly how she had instructed over the phone earlier in the day. Then I swat her again... rub, then swat. Her cheeks are flaming red, her lips parted. I grab the riding crop and begin lightly slapping her with that instead. It is a quicker, but harder sting against her clit and she cries out. I do it again and again. I feel powerful watching the confusion between pleasure and pain cross her face. I give her a brief respite, sticking my mouth on her swollen red clit, licking and sucking. She tastes amazing. I don't want to take my mouth away. I realize it takes just as much discipline to dominate as it does to submit. I bring the riding crop back down, punishing her for how badly I want her. I bring it down on her breasts, her clit, her mouth... everywhere I want to kiss, I swat. Then I cover every inch of her with my mouth. She moans when my lips touch her body. She pants when my mouth returns between her legs, her wetness gushing all over me as I kiss and lick and suck her sex. She is mine now. Completely mine. I feel her submission.

I bring my lips to her mouth and kiss her, long and deep, with my tongue dancing in her mouth. My hands tangle into her silky brown hair and I wrench her head back as she did to me, making her expose her neck to me. I kiss her collarbone. I keep one hand tight in her hair and then slide my other hand down her body and between her legs. I stop at her lips, my fingers resting right against her, but not entering her. "Say it," I breathe between kisses. "Say. It." I am commanding this time.

"Please," she pleads.

I slip two fingers inside her. I have never been inside her before. It has always been me, getting fucked by her. I travel every inch of her, feeling how tight her walls are around me, how unbelievably wet she is for me. I fuck her hard and fast, like she fucked me, my knuckles jamming against her body. I'm inside her as far as I can go. Her arms and legs are tied, but her hips can still move and she slams against me. She comes hard, harder than I thought she would, harder than I thought I could get her to. I slowly withdraw my fingers, not wanting to leave her. Silently I untie her, kissing and rubbing each wrist and ankle as I do so.

"I knew you had it in you." She smiles that smile again. I kiss her in response. I lay down next to her running my hand down her body, stopping at each red mark that the riding crop, that *I*, have caused. Suddenly, my phone alarm goes off. It is my five a.m. wake-up for work.

"I thought you said none of your clients last longer than three hours?" I say, a bemused expression on my face.

"Well, you aren't a client anymore, are you?" She laughs.

"So, I'll wine and dine you at seven tonight then?" I

ask. I'm not timid with her anymore. I say it more like a demand than a request.

"You will." she says, looking me directly in the eyes. "After all, I think we just passed that awkward getting-to-know-you stage, didn't we?" She winks at me and stands up, puts her clothes on, packs her bag, and walks out my door.

# DANCE FOR ME
## JANELLE RESTON

"Again!" she barked, hitting the tip of her cane against the wooden floor. Its *thunk* reverberated through the boards and made the soles of my feet tingle.

I was exhausted. The muscles in my legs and arms quivered like piano strings. But if she wanted me to do it again, so be it. I would give anything to please her.

The accompanist started playing. Professor Lacey thumped her cane faster, goading him up-tempo until his hands flew across the keys at breakneck speed. I felt momentarily sorry for him, until it hit my consciousness that I would have to keep that pace with my entire body, not just my hands. I returned to my starting position at the center of the room.

I'd been dancing for three hours straight—through the ninety-minute group class and now through my weekly private session. Even after seven semesters at a performing arts school, that much dancing was exhausting.

"Your landings are still too heavy, Miranda. If you get it right this time, we're done for the day."

I sucked in my bottom lip, doubting the laws of physics would allow improvement on this front.

Professor Lacey was fluent in body language, and responded as decisively as if I'd spoken my doubts. "I know you don't think you can do it, but *I* know you can. And you will." It was an order as much as a statement of faith. Her eyes were sharp, focused, alive. I felt my strength coming back. My muscles were embers being stoked back into flame.

She tapped the cane against the floor. The movement made her black curls bounce. "On 'four'! One, two, three-and—"

I leapt in the air, then landed as soft as snow. Whether it was the practice or my inability to disobey Professor Lacey's wishes, I couldn't say. I tried not to think about it. Overanalyzing things in the midst of a dance is a sure way to screw up. I surrendered to my body's intelligence and to my teacher: her tapping cane, her commanding voice, the passion she brought to each lesson.

Desire bloomed in my loins. I was flying. I was free.

The dance came to an end. I was on the floor, bent on one knee, my torso pressed against my thigh, my head tucked. I was folded in on myself like a sleeping dove, but my body was supremely awake. I breathed heavily. Blood thrummed through my veins, pounding in my ears. Otherwise, the room was silent.

*Clap. Clap. Clap.*

I looked up. Professor Lacey had her cane tucked under her elbow so she could slap her palms together.

My mind flashed back to the only other time she'd ever clapped for me. It had been early on in the year, when I'd fought her tooth and nail on everything. She'd wanted me to kick higher. I'd given her a long-winded speech about anatomy and the limitations of my own body. When I'd paused long enough to catch my breath, she'd clapped and said with a sneer, "Brava, Miranda. Put that much passion in your acting and maybe someday you'll win a Tony."

Was she mocking me now?

But then I saw her eyes. For the first time since I'd begun working with her, they were alight with unabashed approval. She was smiling so hard it pinched the skin around them into crow's feet. "That was beautiful, Miranda. I knew you could do it. We're done for today."

Exhaustion overtook me again, as well as an unfamiliar emotion: relief. I wanted to crawl the distance between us and kiss her feet. Instead, I stood and gave a curtsy.

She walked toward me. Like the piano earlier, my heartbeat went up-tempo. She rested her hand between my sweat-drenched shoulder blades. "Go to bed early tonight. Your body needs to recover."

* * *

Dancing was not my forte. I'd been a singer first, and then had discovered musical theater. Acting had come easily to me. Dancing? Not so much. I wasn't terrible at it—as a musician, I had no problem moving in time with a beat. But I danced with proficiency, not artistry. My body was tense and inflexible. High kicks and splits were the bane of my existence. I hated being bandied about in some leading man's arms.

I was now at a school for the performing arts in Manhattan, majoring in musical theater. My first three years hadn't been so tough, since my previous dance professors had let me treat the subject as secondary—an accessory to the things I truly cared about. Professor Lacey wouldn't put up with that attitude. She expected me to dance like it was an end in itself. She wanted me to say as much with my body as I could with my voice.

At first, I'd hated her for it. Didn't she understand there were things my body simply couldn't do? Besides, I was destined to be a leading lady, and directors and choreographers constantly make adjustments for their leads' inferior dancing skills. Ethel Merman wasn't expected to be Ginger Rogers. Kristin Chenoweth wasn't Beyoncé.

I'd barged into her office with this argument during the third week of class. I'd just received an email with the grade from my first performance exam with her: D-minus. "This is unacceptable! You're judging me on criteria you'd use for an *actual* dancer. But I'm good enough for musical theater. I know I am!"

My arguments hadn't flown with her. "You don't break into a cut-throat business by being good enough. You do it by blowing people's minds. And that's what I'm going to teach you to do. If you don't want what I'm offering, if it's just too hard for you, talk to your dean. I'm sure she can find some useless filler class to round out your major. You'll have a nice-looking degree to stare at while you wait for calls from your agent that never come."

She'd found my fatal weakness and employed it against me: pride. I was willing to swear eighteen ways to Tuesday that Professor Lacey was unfair in her grading, but no way was I going to admit her class was too hard for me.

So I stuck with it, through all the pain and sweat. I let her break me down, unteaching me the bad habits I'd accumulated through the years. It was the most difficult work of my entire undergraduate career. I learned my body could do things I had never expected. Hannah Lacey pushed me beyond what I thought I was capable of. And I loved her for it.

\* \* \*

I developed the habit of doing everything Professor Lacey told me to, and learned that taking her advice was always to my benefit.

So on the nights she told me to go to bed early, I would —though I didn't always fall asleep right away. I was distracted by images from her studio. Her curly black hair framing her brown face. Her whiskey-colored eyes. Her small breasts, snug in her leotard. Her small hands resting on the large brass knob that topped her dancing cane.

She often wore scarves around her neck. I imagined her unwinding one, holding it out to me like an offering. *Come here, Miranda,* she'd say. I'd walk over to the grand piano, and she'd have me lie on it, my calves dangling over the back leg. She'd tie the scarf around my ankles, binding me to the piano, and then another scarf would appear in her hands, and she would use that to bind my wrists over my head. Then she'd shove off her wrap skirt and pull the crotch of her leotard aside, sinking onto my face, her hot, wet labia pressed against my lips. *Eat*, she'd say, and of course I would, feasting on her dripping pussy as she moaned and writhed. *Good job, Miranda,* she'd moan. *I knew you could do this.* She'd thrust her cunt onto my tongue, her clit against my nose, and as she neared climax she'd reach behind her—a dancer is nothing if not flexible—and slip her fingers into my wetness. She'd come with my name on her lips.

I had some of the best orgasms of my life during these masturbatory sessions, two fingers working furiously over my clit while those of the other hand squeezed at my breasts. They were fierce and overwhelming and, frankly, much more delightful than what Jane, my girlfriend at the time, was giving me. My real sex life was as vanilla as they get. I'd never recognized my own submissive nature until Professor Lacey awoke it. But it didn't occur to me to pursue her. She seemed far off, unreachable. Besides, I was pretty sure it was against the rules.

"Tie me up," I said one evening to Jane. We were in her bed, our clothes halfway off.

She looked at me like I'd gone crazy. "Why would I do that?"

"I just—I thought it would be fun to try. That's all."

To Jane's credit, she tried. But the energy was all wrong. "It feels weird when you can't touch me back," she said. "And how am I supposed to get off?"

"You could sit on my face."

She squinched her nose. "But that's so demeaning."

*That's the idea,* I wanted to say, but didn't. It wasn't Jane I wanted demeaning me, anyway. It was Professor Lacey. I wanted to give myself over to her completely—not just my dancing, but all of me. I wanted her to take me apart and build me back up again, make me more whole than I was before.

* * *

A week before graduation, I went out with a group of friends to celebrate the completion of exams. Jane and I had broken up by then—the vanilla sex had become unbearable to me, and my demands for kink had become unbearable to her—and I was hoping the night would end with me getting laid by a powerful stranger.

I hadn't gotten all my grades back yet, but I knew I'd done well enough that my degree was in no danger. Professor Lacey's class was the most challenging, and even she had given me an approving smile when I finished my routine for her, though this time she had not clapped. "You've grown so much this year," she'd said at the conclusion of my dance. "It's been an honor to watch you bloom."

She was, of course, the reason for my blossoming. She was the sun and rain. Without her, I couldn't have grown.

My desire to find a fuckable stranger flew out the window as soon as my group walked into the bar and I spotted Professor Lacey in the corner, sharing drinks with another woman around her age. Professor Lacey's companion looked like she might be a dancer too, with a wiry body and long blonde hair cascading down her back. The blonde batted her eyes and laughed enthusiastically whenever Professor Lacey spoke, but Professor Lacey didn't return the enthusiasm. She seemed distracted. She fiddled with the ends of her own silk scarf, her eyes flitting around the room until, at last, they landed on me.

Her mouth spread into a smile. I waved. She winked at me. My stomach flipped.

She turned back to her companion, and the moment was suddenly gone. I wondered if it had occurred at all. Perhaps it had been a product of my horny imagination.

My friends and I found a table. I had one margarita and then another. My eyes scanned the bar as restlessly as Professor Lacey's had done when I'd first entered. They often wandered to her, and to the blonde, who was ramping up her flirtations. Every few minutes, she reached across the table to readjust Professor Lacey's purple scarf or touch her hand. Jealousy burned my throat.

As I finished my third margarita, Professor Lacey walked over to the bar. The blonde checked her phone, then rifled through a purse for a small mirror, which she peered at in the dim light to apply lipstick.

I slammed my glass down on the table, excused myself to my friends, and made a beeline to the bar.

"Professor Lacey! What a surprise to see you here!" My head felt woozy and my chest warm. These sensations only increased when Professor Lacey turned away from the bartender to face me head on. Her lips curled, as if she were trying to stifle a laugh. I didn't know how I felt about that. I liked to see her happy, but I didn't want her laughing at my expense.

"I'm not drunk, if that's what you're thinking. I'm just happy to see you."

Professor Lacey's smile grew. "I'm happy to see you, too. Though usually when people start off a conversation with, 'I'm not drunk,' it means they are."

I was too thrilled by her first statement to be offended by her second. Professor Lacey was happy to see *me*. Perhaps it was the first glimpse of happiness she'd had all night. Perhaps she would take me home with her, and I could give her even more.

The bartender set a drink in front of Professor Lacey. I pulled out my wallet. "Let me buy your drink, professor."

She put a hand on my wrist to stop me from opening the wallet. It was a light touch, but commanding. "No, thank you, Miranda. That wouldn't be appropriate. I haven't turned in all your grades yet."

I glanced back at her table as she gave the bartender a ten. The blonde was watching us. I waved, as if to assure her I was no threat, though I hoped I was. An idea popped in my head—one that would satisfy my curiosity about the blonde woman's status, and that might also convince Professor Lacey to accept some sort of gift from me. "Is that your date? I can buy her a drink, instead of you. *She's* not grading me."

"She's not my date. And don't fool yourself into thinking I can't see right through why you asked me that." Her smile disappeared. It turned grim, disciplinary—the way it had always turned when I wasn't performing up to her standards. "I don't fuck my students, Miranda."

If she'd slapped me across the face, it would have stung less. But I wasn't going to give up so easily. I reached out and curled my fingers around the end of her scarf. It was one I'd seen many times. Batiked deep purple, it seemed almost as much a part of her body as her brown skin. "I've always thought this scarf would look so pretty tied around my wrists."

I didn't look away from her eyes. There seemed to be a struggle going on behind them, but the rest of her face remained impassive. "Be that as it may, you are still my student and you've had too much to drink."

"I'm not too drunk to know what I want."

"By any legal definition, I'm afraid you are, darling." She took her drink and held it up as if in a toast. "Congratulations on your impending graduation, Miranda. I look forward to seeing you on Broadway." She turned and walked back to the blonde.

I collapsed onto a bar stool, my eyes not moving from her though she refused to look my way again. She had called me *darling*. She'd implicitly agreed her scarf would look lovely on my wrists. She thought I was headed for Broadway.

It was the best rejection I'd ever received. I went back to my friends, had a few more drinks, and looked forward to masturbating myself to sleep when I got home. After graduation, I'd make another move on Professor Lacey, and she would say yes.

But when I woke up the next morning with a headache like an axe to the skull, the conversation's meaning seemed altogether different. She hadn't agreed I'd look nice tied up in her scarf; she'd simply avoided disagreeing. Her *darling* had been a dismissal, not an endearment. *I look forward to seeing you on Broadway* wasn't exactly an invitation to keep in close touch. She'd barely held back a sneer.

I'd bought a thank-you card to send to her at graduation, to thank her for the ways in which she'd changed my perceptions of my own abilities, for driving me to do better than I'd thought possible.

But what I'd really wanted to say was *I love you and don't want to live without you.*

She could clearly live without me. I threw the card away.

* * *

I did my best to forget about her, though it was impossible to let go of her completely. She'd become part of my muscle memory, of the way I moved whenever I danced.

I met women who were willing to tie me up, spank me, flog me, gag me—to push me past the boundaries that had held me in before. I fell in love with none of them, and none of them fell in love with me. When they disciplined me, I often imagined Professor Lacey's voice in place of theirs, her wooden dance cane in place of their whips and riding crops. My body and heart thrived on the attention all the same.

I made it into a Broadway chorus line, then as an understudy for one of the show's supporting cast members. A few months later, I got the call from my agent that would change my life in more ways than one: I'd gotten the lead in an off-off-Broadway musical that was moving to off-Broadway. My agent told me my dancing was what had made me stand out in callbacks.

I was on the bus, squeezed between an old lady with a

collapsible grocery cart and a skinny kid who smelled like patchouli. My heart thudded in my chest. Throughout callbacks, I'd pretended I was dancing for Professor Lacey. It was a trick I used frequently in auditions. Picturing her eyes on me, hearing her thumping cane with each beat—they both soothed my nerves and made me perform better than I thought possible.

I had to tell her. I had to thank her. Even if I wasn't a necessary fixture in her life, she had changed mine for the better. Thirty seconds later I was outside, running to the subway, zipping toward Manhattan and my alma mater.

Running back to her.

The building was open when I got there, students milling in the halls. But the studio was empty, and her office door closed.

I knocked.

"Who is it?" It was her voice, clear and self-possessed as always.

"Miranda Jamison."

A chair screeched against the wooden floor. A lock tumbled. The door opened.

Professor Lacey looked exactly as I remembered her: leotard snug to her subtle curves, the purple silk scarf from that night at the bar, a skirt wrapped around her boyish hips.

She also looked nothing like I remembered. The expression on her face was one I had never seen before— pained and straining, like she was fighting back hope. She held herself rigidly, inflexible as the dance cane that leaned against the wall, its spherical brass handle glinting in the window's light. "Miranda, come in." Her breath was fast, shallow. She gestured for me to sit on the couch and locked the door behind me. "It's good to see you. Surprising, but good."

I didn't sit. I couldn't. Adrenaline pounded in my veins. "Professor Lacey—"

"Call me Hannah. You're not a student anymore." That

kind of invitation ought to be filled with warmth, but her voice and eyes were cold.

"Hannah. I got a musical lead. Off-Broadway. And I wanted to thank you, because I never did—"

Her cold demeanor evaporated. She threw her arms around me—the first time she'd ever done so—and pulled me close. I felt her breasts against mine, her heart beating against my ribcage. She kissed my cheek. "There's nothing to thank me for. You did all the work."

"I only did the work because you dared me to." I tried to shrug the kiss off as a meaningless gesture, but my body didn't get the memo. It thrummed with electricity and desire. I turned my face instinctively, pressing my lips against hers.

She responded immediately, opening her mouth, sucking hard on my bottom lip, then tugging it between her teeth. I moaned, clutching my hands around her shoulders like she was a life preserver. Soon I was pressed against the desk, Hannah's hands curling into my ass. My hips stuttered. Something fell clattering to the floor.

Hannah startled back. "Miranda—" She was breathless.

"Don't stop kissing me." I tugged at the ends of her scarf. She stepped toward me—not unwillingly, but not eagerly, either. Her face was a question mark. "Please, Professor... Hannah. I've wanted you ever since I stopped hating you."

Her mouth quirked into a smile. "You really did hate me for a while, didn't you?"

I nodded. "Until I realized I needed the guidance of someone who was willing to break me." I looked into her dark, unblinking eyes. "I still do. Do you want to do that for me, Hannah? Do you want me to submit myself to you?"

"Oh, god, yes." She surged toward me, closing the last inches between us, her delicate dancer's fingers on my jaw and neck. "I've wanted that with you since *before* you stopped hating me."

I would have laughed, but her lips were against mine,

almost violent in their need. She pried my teeth open with her tongue, pushed herself into my mouth: took me, possessed me. Her hands were everywhere: my face and neck, my hair, my breasts, my ass. She tugged at the hem of my sweater and pulled it up, revealing the utilitarian beige bra beneath. I cursed myself for not planning ahead, but my shame didn't last long. She tugged it off along with the shirt and threw them both to the floor, taking one breast in her hand and pulling my nipple into her mouth with a hard suck.

Pleasure shot to my toes. I yelped my approval.

"There are people in the hallway, Miranda. Am I going to have to gag you?"

"Yes, do, please," I whispered breathlessly, my arousal ratcheting up past its earlier limits.

Hannah smirked and stepped back. "Fine, then. But I don't have any gags at the ready here. We'll have to improvise." With that, she hauled me onto the desk, pulling down my jeans and panties so that I was stripped bare, my back and ass against the cool wood, the rest of me exposed to the air. Goosebumps prickled on my skin.

"Before I gag you—" She leaned over me, kissing me fiercely as I wrapped my bare legs around her waist, pressing my clit against her pubic bone. Through the fabric of her leotard, I felt her nipples growing hard and pebbled against my own breasts.

I tugged again at her scarf. "Please, professor. Don't you think this scarf would look better tied around my wrists?"

"You vixen," she muttered into my neck. "Do you know how hard it was not to take you that night at the bar? The way you looked at me—you were practically begging for it."

"Not *practically*. I *was* begging for it. I wanted you to fuck me, professor. I wanted you to own me."

"And don't think I don't notice you 'professor'-ing me. I know what you're up to."

"What am I up to?" I thrust my clit against her pubic bone again, seeking more friction.

"You're playing the pervy little schoolgirl, Miranda. Are you looking for a spanking?"

"I can't say I'd mind one."

She slid down and walked around the desk, slipping off her scarf. "Wrists above your head, my darling." Wetness gushed from my cunt at the endearment, and again at the feeling of her silk scarf pressing against my wrists. She made the binding snug but not overly tight—she was clearly experienced at this—then pressed something cold and metallic into one of my palms. "Keys," she said in response to my questioning look. "Drop them if you need to stop. Because you won't be able to say 'red' around these." She lifted my panties to my face. They smelled strongly of my arousal. "This is your gag, my darling Miranda. Now open your mouth and bite down." I did. The silken fabric was wet and slick. I wished it was her I tasted, and not me. Perhaps she would give me that gift later, if I was good for her.

"Now spread your legs. I want to get a good view of your beautiful cunt. I've wanted to taste it since you first back-talked to me."

I planted my feet wide on the desk, my knees in the air. I felt deliciously exposed as she traced the tips of her fingers over my labia. I bit into my panties to keep from grunting out my pleasure. "What a juicy pink pussy, Miranda. So wet for me. Did you always get this wet when you performed for me?" She slid two fingers into my desperate cunt. "Watching you dance always got me wet, darling—seeing you work so hard for my approval. Sometimes I'd have to come here into my office and fuck myself afterward just to get on with the day."

I churned my hips, seeking friction against my G-spot.

"Not yet, darling. I need to tell you something else. You know my dancing cane?"

I nodded against the desk.

"Can you guess how many times I've gotten off to the thought of fucking you with the brass handle? Would you like that, darling? Would you like to polish it with your cunt?"

I moaned around my wadded panties. That cane was as much a part of her as her hand or tongue. To have it inside my body, filling and stretching me, would be a dream come true. I spread my legs a little more, and she worked three fingers in.

"I bet you've dreamed about me disciplining you with it, too, haven't you? I saw the way you used to look at it, darling, like you were afraid of it and wanted it at the same time. Was I reading you right, sweet Miranda?"

I nodded again, groaning around the gag. I lifted my ass off the table, ready to expose myself to her beatings.

She merely gave it a light slap—a promise of pain rather than the thing itself. "Not today. Right now, I want to make love to you. Will you let me do that?"

I answered by fucking myself onto her fingers. She curled the pads against my G-spot, rubbing it in smooth, irresistible circles. My cunt spasmed; my eyes rolled back in my head. I was right on the edge of coming, if only she would press her thumb to my clit or pinch my nipple with her free hand.

Instead, she slipped her fingers out. "I'm not letting you come yet, darling. I haven't waited this long to fuck you for it to be all over."

She stepped back. I craned my neck to watch her. She unwrapped the skirt from her waist and dropped it to the floor, then unpeeled her leotard and tights from her skin. Beneath them was a black cotton bra and panties, which she left on as she grabbed the cane from its resting place by the wall. She smoothed her hands over the brass globe at the top before stretching it out to me, rolling it over my nipples and belly, my ass and thighs, my neck and arms. The metal was cold at first, but grew less so as she soothed it over my skin.

I closed my eyes and luxuriated in the sensation. It was as sensual as kisses, as erotic as a lover's tongue exploring the crevices of my body. Each touch made me shiver with longing, made my cunt grow hungrier with desire.

"Take me", I tried to beg around the panties in my mouth, but the words came out as a garbled moan.

"You'd like me to fuck you, wouldn't you, Miranda? You feel like you can't possibly stand another minute without something in your cunt."

I nodded desperately, close to tears.

She rolled the handle over my gaping pussy lips—a tease more than a relief. "I think you can stand it, Miranda. If I ask you to stand it, you'll rise to the occasion, won't you?"

I took a deep breath, let her will become my own. I kept my hips still as she continued to roll the knob over my labia, coating it in my juices. I willed my cunt not to quiver, not even when she added to the torture by dipping her head down and sucking my hard nipple into an even harder peak. "Oh, Miranda," she moaned, "your tits are to die for."

The compliment made me flush and forget my own desire. So when the brass sphere pushed suddenly into my pussy, it was a shock bordering on revelation. I spasmed hungrily around it, pulling it in until the cool brass nuzzled my G-spot. Tears of ecstasy streamed down my face. I grasped the keys so tightly that the teeth cut into my skin—but better that than dropping them to the floor. There was no way I was going to let that happen now, not when Hannah had me right where she wanted me.

She wiped the tears from my cheeks. "You're doing so well, sweetheart. I'll let you come soon. But first, I want to take this gag out of your mouth and replace it with my cunt. Would you like that?"

I nodded eagerly, holding back my whimper as she pulled the cane's brass knob from my cunt and licked it like a lollipop. "You taste like honey, Miranda. Do you want to know what I taste like?" She removed the gag.

"Yes, professor. Please. Please let me taste your cunt." She stood up to remove her panties and bra. Her nipples were as dark as her eyes and bigger than silver dollars. My mouth watered at the sight, but I was soon distracted by something even more tempting as she climbed onto the desk, her knees on either side of my shoulders and her face resting against my raised knee. Her cunt hovered about a foot above my face, its lips engorged and glistening with arousal. I struggled to lift my head so I could taste it, but with my wrists tied above me, it was impossible to get enough purchase.

"Patience," Hannah chided as she inserted the brass globe back into my cunt.

"Oh god!"

"Shhhh."

"I'd be quieter if you sat on my face," I muttered.

"You do have a point." She sank down, aligning her cunt over my outstretched tongue, grinding her clit against my chin. She smelled of sweat and tasted like sugar and butter, melting just as easily on my probing tongue. "Yes, Miranda, eat me just like that." She bit my knee with a stifled cry.

Her clit swelled against my chin. I pulled my tongue from her cunt and lapped it down onto her hard nub, sweeping back and forth between the two, aided by her vigorous rocking. Inside my own cunt, the brass sphere seemed to be spinning against my G-spot. I quivered around it, ready to melt.

"Miranda," she muttered, "I'm so close. Do you want to come with me?"

I couldn't answer except by fucking her more vigorously with my tongue and working myself over the brass sphere.

Suddenly her tongue was on my clit, lapping eagerly as she continued to press her cunt into my face. Her labia fluttered, and then her whole body. She moaned, sending sparks up my spine. I cried into her cunt, coming with my whole body as she gushed creamy wetness into my mouth and over my chin.

I came for what seemed like ages, my body refusing to stop even as she pulled the brass handle from inside me and dropped it to the floor. "Not bad for our first time together," she said as she rolled off and rearranged herself so she was lying next to me on the wide desk, her head pressed against my shoulder. "I can't wait to see what our second time is like. And the times after that."

I kissed her. Our juices mingled on our tongues. "I probably have a hundred fantasies I'd like to try out with you, if it wouldn't be a bother."

She smiled. "Do any of them involve me fucking you in the dance studio? Because I have one about tying you to the baby grand that I'd love to try sometime, now that you're no longer my student."

I smiled. "Great minds think alike."

# SERIOUS SWIMMER
## J. BELLE LAMB

You think the women's locker room is empty, so you peel off your swimsuit without worrying about who may be watching. You swam hard today, adding ten laps to your workout, and all you want is a quick shower before you head home. The water in the communal shower is hot, its warmth needling your sore muscles.

But the locker room isn't empty after all. She's there when you step out of the shower, towel wrapped carefully around your body. You wonder if she saw you showering, but she seems intent on pulling her own suit off, and you decide that as long as you're careful with your towel, you'll avoid letting her see you naked.

So you do a careful dance, bent over so that the towel drapes around you as you face your locker and rub lotion into your skin. You wiggle into your bra and tuck the towel back around your body to pull underwear on underneath it, then drop your loose dress over it, finally letting the towel fall to the floor once you're mostly covered. She's taken her own quick shower while you've done this dance, and is unselfconsciously naked as she's drying off. You notice a tattoo on her thigh as she gets dressed, a snake, or a dragon, maybe, and then you remind yourself that you shouldn't be looking. Still, as you pull on your leggings, and then socks and boots, you sneak another peek and realize she's really attractive, short dark hair wet and spiky, the muscles of a serious swimmer lining her shoulders and legs.

You decide to skip any primping you might otherwise do before heading out. You're not going anywhere but home, and though you like to be well groomed, you want to get out of here just in case Serious Swimmer did get a look at you naked. You pack your bag, wet swimsuit, towel and toiletries, and walk out of the locker room, avoiding looking in her direction.

You're all the way to your car before you hear footsteps behind you. Keys in hand, you jump when you hear her voice.

"Hey. Sorry to startle you," she says. You turn to look at her. Up close, she's even more attractive: laugh lines at the corners of dark eyes, a kind smile above her loose black sweatshirt. She's just taller enough that you have to tip your chin to meet her gaze.

"That's okay," you say. You're dreading what comes next, the inevitable conversation with the concerned citizen about abuse, the questions she may ask directly or may hint at.

"I just was wondering," she says, a twinkle coming into her eyes, "if you don't mind me asking: flogger or cane?"

The ground lurches under you for a moment and you drop your keys. She bends down to pick them up, putting them back into your hand and gently closing your fingers over them.

"Sorry... I..." you try.

"You were expecting something different. Again, I apologize for startling you. I saw the marks while you were showering. They're nice work."

"I... it was a flogger," you finally say. "Lots of fun."

"Nice! Good to know someone's taking care of you," she says, a sharpness creeping into her smile. "I'm Lane."

"Trixie." You shake the hand she's offering.

"Trixie. Trouble." Her smile widens. "Well, Trouble, I hope I'll see you around." As she walks away, muscular ass filling out a pair of jeans painfully well, you regain sense enough to feel your heart slamming against your ribs, but you still cannot make words come out of your mouth.

After about a car's length, she turns, a truly wicked grin lighting up her face. "Oh, and Trixie—next time, use one of the family changing rooms." You must look as dumbfounded as you feel because she chuckles as she disappears into the parking lot.

* * *

Weeks pass and you don't see her again. You've written it off as a chance encounter, maybe even a hallucination brought on by inhaling too much swimming pool chlorine. Your life proceeds in its usual rhythms: home, work, to the pool twice a week to swim. The bruises that Lane saw on your ass fade and are replaced with fresh bruises on your breasts and thighs. The hope that now accompanies your workouts is the only thing new in your world. You remember to shower in the family changing rooms. Just in case.

And then one day, through fogged goggles, you see something on an upstroke. A thigh tattooed with a snake. Or a dragon. You still can't tell. But you're sure it's her, swimming in the next lane over. You inhale water and almost choke, flailing inelegantly, not sure if you're laughing at the pun—lane and Lane—or suddenly so turned on you can't remember how to swim.

You wonder if she recognizes you. You have a tattoo as well, hummingbirds and flowers on your left arm, but you don't know if she saw it. And your swimsuit is different, a new suit that covers more of your breasts and ass.

She's swimming laps, moving aggressively through the water in a butterfly stroke, one you've never mastered. Short of ducking under the lane markers to swim directly into her you can't think of a way to get her attention; besides, interrupting her workout would be rude.

So you swim, trying to let the water work its magic of erasing all thought beyond the rhythmic counting you've always done while swimming, starting with one at the pool's edge and ending the count at its opposite end: *One, two, three, four. She is so hot. Maybe I could just wait in the locker room.*

*Dammit. Where was I? Seven, eight, eleven. Would it be too forward to ask her for a drink? Twenty, twenty-one, that was not a big enough breath. Is she watching me swim? Dammit. Just swim, already!*

You give up after your minimum workout, too distracted to push for the extra laps you'd intended. Lane's still pushing hard, those shoulders practically catapulting her body out of the water with every stroke. You watch for a few moments from the shallow end, but it's getting busy in the pool, people starting to fill and even double up in the lap lanes, so you get out, abandoning your place to someone else.

You try to shake the subtle sense of heartbreak that follows you into the locker room, where you duck down the hallway to the family changing rooms. It's not really heartbreak, just the sharp frustration of a connection lost, like missing the last step in a set of stairs and stumbling your way onto solid ground. You get your towel and backpack out of your locker.

Your hand is on the door to Family Changing Room number three when she steps up behind you, putting her hand above yours to push the door open. Lane says nothing, following you into the little concrete and tile room. You stay silent, afraid that if you open your mouth, what certainly must be a chlorine-induced dream will end. You set your bag and towel on the little room's bench; she drops her own bag and towel next to yours. You hear the door's lock click shut.

You turn. She's right there, still dripping wet from the pool. You can see now that the tattoo is a dragon, serpentine body picked out in green and red on her thigh. Its head rests right under her hipbone, tongue flicking toward her crotch.

"Strip," she says. Your heart has begun to slam against your ribs again. You don't even think about doing anything else and soon your suit is lying in a sodden pile on the floor.

She reaches into the shower stall and turns on the water. You can't take your eyes off her as she peels out of her own suit, tossing it next to yours. Her breasts are lovely, a little larger than your small handfuls, and she keeps her pubic hair neatly trimmed.

Lane looks at you for a moment, eyes gleaming as she picks out the bruises on your breasts and inner thighs. She steps close to run her fingers over the chain of inch-long bruises that follow the line of your breasts. "Teeth?"

"Some. And clothespins." Your voice sounds strange to you, as if you're standing next to your body as you speak. The hiss of the shower fills the little room.

Lane reaches down to touch your thighs, tapping the inside of your leg to make you move your feet apart so she can trace the bigger bruises there. "Same here?"

"Yes. Fists, too."

"You play rough." Still tracing the bruises on your thighs, her fingers are so close to your cunt that you want to beg her to put them inside you now, right now.

"Yes. Just part of who I am."

"Beautiful," she says, and then her hand is in your wet hair, holding your head as she kisses you. It's a demanding kiss, as if Lane has suddenly become aware that other people have been enjoying something she wants. You're glad your back is already against the tile wall because otherwise you would melt to the floor.

She kisses you there, moving to pin you against the wall, her dragon in between your thighs, her hand in your hair. She finds the bruises on your breasts with her free hand and pinches them, making you writhe against her as the sharp flashes of pain burn into pleasure.

Lane breaks the kiss to look at you, eyes locked on yours. "Trixie," she says, "I've been looking forward to seeing you again." She kisses the side of your neck, nipping lightly, and you gasp. "I want to fuck you," she growls in your ear. "Is that all right?"

"Yes," you say, "please."

She dips her head to find your breast, taking your nipple in her mouth and sucking it, gently at first, then harder as you moan and shiver against her. She switches sides, fingers pinching where her mouth just was, both of your nipples quickly blooming into bright points of pleasure.

Lane moves back to kiss you, letting go of your hair to cup your face, the gesture sweet and possessive. "Stay there," she tells you, and you do, still grateful for the wall's solidity. She reaches into her backpack to pull out a Ziploc bag: gloves and lube.

"Planning ahead?" you ask, watching her snap on the black nitrile gloves.

"A few weeks ago I met a beautiful woman at the pool," she says, stepping close to run her gloved hands over your thighs. "I believe in being prepared." And then she's reaching a hand to find your clit, working it hard enough to make you need to grasp her shoulders for balance as the dizzying rush of pleasure sweeps through you.

"Will you come for me like this, Trixie?" she asks, lips close to your ear, her free hand reaching up between your bodies to pinch the bruises on your breast again. You bury your head against her neck in response, trying not to cry out as you come, lightning searing through you from her lips to your breast to your clit and back again.

She lets the orgasm peak and settle. "What a lovely treat you are, Trixie," she says, slipping first one, then two fingers into your slick cunt. She fucks you in earnest, fingers thrusting deep inside you to reach for your G-spot as her thumb puts pressure on your clit. She lets you keep your face buried against her shoulder, the shower's hiss not quite loud enough to keep your muffled cries from filling the small room.

You come, long and hard, the orgasm thrilling in its rawness. Lane doesn't stop, pushing your thighs further open with her knee so that she can use the wall to lift you, jamming your deeply bruised thighs against her body. It hurts, hot red pain pounding through your thighs to mix with the electric pleasure of being expertly fucked.

"Give it all to me, beautiful," she growls in your ear and then bites you hard, right where the line of your neck meets the curve of your shoulder. You're choking again, flailing now in a rush of pain and pleasure instead of the pool's deep end, and you sob against her.

When you come, you feel like you're falling through the air, buffeted by hard winds. Your cunt spasms around her fingers, fluid pouring from you to smear her glove and drip onto the concrete floor, and your heart threatens to break a rib. Lane's good enough to bear down on your neck for one last second as the orgasm starts to fade, tearing a fresh cry from you.

She holds you there for a few moments as you shake, ripples of pleasure and pain still fizzing through you. She kisses you, still possessive, still hungry, but sweet now as she takes her fingers from your cunt and eases your feet back onto the floor.

Lane peels off her gloves and then smoothes your tousled hair back from your forehead. "We'd better shower quickly," she says, and pulls you into the water's spray.

# CALL FOR SUBMISSION
## ELNA HOLST

Selma took one last look at the burning orange letters that spelled out BOOKSHOP in the window, before turning them off for the night. The familiar ache in her lower back mingled with the sweet taste of pride in another night's book circle passed with flying colors. The lecturer from the local college had gushed at their generosity for hosting these events, gushed about Carol Ann Duffy, and been in a state which could only be described as on the verge of delirium on the topic of 'Warming Her Pearls'. The exuberant redhead had blushed vehemently as Selma smiled, leaned her head to the side and handed her a fresh batch of their discreet calling-cards. She promised to hand them out to everyone in her new class for the term. Business thrived.

Selma smiled again, and silently scolded herself. She was a hopeless flirt. It *was* good for business though, and Edith never seemed to mind. Whenever she caught her at it, she would just raise her eyebrows slightly and look at her over the translucent frames of those reading glasses she insisted on wearing, and Selma would know, as she always knew, deep down, that she was bound. Body, heart and soul.

Brushing ginger out of her mind, Selma went to lock the rickety stained-glass door that led to the stairs to the street outside. Their small second-hand bookshop lay in an austere red-brick building, half a floor below ground level, which was the only reason she had finally consented to let Edith put up that gaudy fluorescent sign.

"It's tacky!" she had exclaimed, a note of desperation apparent in her otherwise well-modulated voice.

To which Edith had blithely averred: "It's kitschy. Don't worry. They'll love it. Besides, we do need to call attention to ourselves down here." She had turned her head as she was putting it up, to see the doubtful look on her partner's face. She snaked an arm around her waist, whispering in her ear, "You'll get used to it. Give it a week. Then we'll take it down again, if you want." Selma had stroked Edith's corduroy-clad rump, giving it a sharp pinch that made the miscreant yelp and laugh. After that, Edith had been a very good girl indeed, for the entire week. The sign remained.

Selma stretched, lynxlike, to alleviate the soreness of her tired limbs. She stacked the empty chairs up at the back of the shop, swearing under her breath at the pang of pain when one of them scuffed her toe. Where the hell was Edith anyway? It wasn't like her not to come up and help close shop.

She gazed around the twilit space, usually so cheerful with its inundation of books, stacked in cases, packed along the shelves, towering in yet-to-be-sorted piles, mingling with random curiosities and bric-a-brac. Now, it looked almost sinister, with the deepening shadows; there was a near tangible sense of something missing, when not a single being browsed the aisles. The quaint little mantelpiece clock by the till struck ten and Selma all but jumped out of her own skin.

Her annoyance grew. Damn that silly old clock. And damned woman for disappearing on her. What was it she had said again? Something about books. Oh, *the* books, she recalled now, Edith was supposed to have gone to finish this month's bookkeeping in the office downstairs. Selma frowned. She opened the squeaky wooden door to the basement and peered down. She couldn't hear a thing from down there, but through the otherwise compact darkness of the hallway, she could just make out the thin strip of light from under the closed door to the office. Surely, she must have finished by now? Selma flicked the light switch by the top of the stairs. Nothing happened. She flicked it another four times, just to be sure. No.

The bulbs had conveniently burned out all at once.

Swearing in earnest now, Selma threaded her way back to the counter, and got the spare torch from the drawer under the till. Switching it on, and quietly blessing the benign goddesses of Luck and Chance that these batteries, at least, were in working order, she pointed the light source back in the direction she had come from, and made for the basement once more.

Selma padded lightly down the wooden staircase, worn soft and sloping by centuries of use. As she went down, she was passing into the oldest part of the building. It always gave her a thrill, thinking of all the feet and their respective owners, in whose steps she trod. As though she was part of an age-old line of store owners and shopkeepers, linked together not by blood but by the place itself; something of each of them bleeding into the walls, leaving their indelible marks in wood and stone, even after their mortal dust had long since scattered and decayed.

Selma took care not to make the floorboards creak as she came down into the hallway. Gold and bronze-embossed letters glinted at her from the finer antiquarian volumes they stored down here as she swung the light over the shelves, approaching the office door. Standing before it, Selma turned off her torch and bent to peek through the keyhole. She could see next to nothing, of course. Just light and moving shadows. But finally, she heard little rustling noises which she supposed must be Edith, leafing through the pages of some file. The familiar sound calmed her, lulled her. She shook herself. Being placated without even having crossed the threshold was not part of her plan. She felt for her keys in her skirt pocket and fitted the right one in place. Quickly, she turned the lock and let herself in, banging the door shut behind her.

The woman inside gasped, her silver pen falling from her hand. She was sitting at the monumental work desk, looking more than a touch disheveled. Her short hair stood on end, and she had stripped down to her green racerback tank top, her cardigan thrown in a pile on the floor. An ambiguous, but rather triumphant smile crossed Selma's face as she studied her prey.

"Where's the ledger?" she inquired, knowing the answer to her question already.

Edith blushed. Her hand came up to stroke her neck. "Eh," she managed.

"Still upstairs by the counter, I presume?" Selma stalked closer, basking in the tension that suddenly filled the room. "You haven't been doing any accounting at all, have you?" She went up to stand behind her, putting her hands comfortably on Edith's shoulders, leaning over her. "Oh my," Selma tutted, reading a sentence here and there from the handwritten pages strewn across the table. "Someone's been an awfully bad girl."

The muscles in Edith's neck tensed as Selma increased the pressure on her shoulders. Selma tutted again, running her fingers up into Edith's hair, pulling at the tangles. Edith winced and shuddered at the minute mixture of pleasure and pain, hands balled into fists in her lap. Selma smiled to herself, admiring her partner's laudable potential for self-restraint. She knew Ed was stronger than her, maybe even twice as strong. In fact, her uncanny reserves of power had surprised and defeated scores of cocky opponents during her stint as a competitive armwrestler.

Selma could still conjure up the frisson of clandestine arousal which had flooded her, sitting at the back of the audience, hearing the judge call out "Straps!" whenever sweaty palms slid apart before the match was over. As they bound Edith's hand to that of some unwitting woman, Selma had nearly had to do the same to her own, knotting them into the scarf in her lap to refrain from touching herself. "Yes, you can borrow her for now," she had muttered under her breath. "That ass is mine tonight." Edith wrestled her opponent's arm to the table with nonchalant ease, and Selma's gut tightened with desire.

"I had to write," Edith mumbled, head lowered, shoulders hunched. "There was this call for submission."

Her voice trailed off and Selma pushed the recollection aside, focusing on the flesh-and-blood version of her lover. Yes, straps, she thought. And that candle the little vixen had seen fit to light in the heavy bronze candlestick on the mantelpiece. She, too, felt inspired by the muses tonight.

"I see," she replied, gathering up the offending pages of the manuscript and clearing the rough surface of the work desk. She pocketed Edith's discarded glasses that were lying perilously close to the edge of the left-hand side. "A call for submission. Indeed. And did you ask for permission to flippantly neglect your duties and lock yourself in here for such frivolities?"

Edith shook her head, fingers fidgeting with the edge of her provocative tank top.

"Did you lie, on purpose, about what you were doing down here?"

Edith shook her head again, more vigorously. She cleared her throat.

"I... I did intend to do the books, too. They're... They should be here somewhere. I just got side-tracked."

"Side-tracked." Selma dipped into the bottom drawer of the desk, snatching up the long disused armwrestler's straps. Edith's eyes widened, then quickly narrowed. The tips of her ears took on a charming russet nuance.

"I know just the remedy for that," Selma continued, tying the straps to the big brass rings that hung from the short side of the desk. She glanced over her shoulder at Edith. "Undress, please."

Not stopping to see if she was being obeyed, she went to fetch her foldable music stand from over by the ruddy oak bookcase. Arranging it just in front of her set-up with the rings and straps, she put the reams of scribbled notes on it as though it were sheet music. Turning back, she found Edith standing compliantly by the table, her corduroy

45

trousers and tank top neatly folded on the seat she had vacated.

Her small, pert breasts were puckered from the sudden cool. A telling stain had formed at the front of her white cotton knickers. Selma raised her eyebrows. Edith slipped off the panties, her movements awkward with anticipation. Selma felt the yearning echoed in her own nether regions. She couldn't resist walking up to her, pressing herself lightly against the sheepish nude from behind, kissing her neck, running her tongue behind her ear before she whispered into it, "You do look juicy. I'd have liked to have tasted that, had you not been such an insubordinate minx."

Edith leant back against her, her breathing jagged. "Please," she said hoarsely, her muscles taut with reining in her growing excitement.

"But you haven't really earned that, have you?"

"I'll make amends," Edith begged. "Whatever you want. I'll stay up and crunch numbers all night."

"Maybe you will," Selma murmured, her hands appraising her lover's arse, squeezing the firm orbs like putty. "But in my experience, you respond swiftest to physical education."

Edith was all but gagging for it.

"Bend over the desk, honey. I've cleared it for you."

As Edith followed her instructions, Selma tightened the straps around her wrists, pausing briefly to admire the tableau she had created. Edith was standing on tip-toes to reach across the length of the table, her trim torso pushing into the wood, her arms fastened securely, cheek resting on the surface. There was a nice stretch to her legs and buttocks, the slightest of quivers to that tight, sinewy flesh giving away the strain that was already building up.

"No, no," said Selma, catching her lover's chin and raising her head from the wooden surface, nimbly producing Edith's reading spectacles from her skirt pocket and sliding them on her. She fiddled the temple tips in place behind her ears, stroking some stray hairs from Ed's sweetly perspiring face. "I want you to see what you have done as I deliver your punishment. In fact, I'd like you to read it out for me. Can you see from here?"

She noticed a gratifying hint of panic in the offender's eyes. Edith licked her dry lips, stalling for time.

"It's a very rough draft," she objected weakly.

"Oh good," Selma cooed, fetching the burning candle she had spied, taking care to protect the flame. "I like it rough."

"What are you—"

"Never you mind. Read." Selma went to stand at her side, knitting the fingers of her free hand into Edith's hair once more, holding her head up so she was forced to look straight ahead at the text in front of her. She held the candle poised, just above the top of her beautifully exposed spine.

"It was a dark and stormy night," Edith intoned, "in the year of our Lord, 1830."

Selma tilted the candle ever so slightly, letting a drop of hot candle wax fall onto the top vertebra of Edith's spinal cord.

"Oh." Ed's sharp intake of breath revealed a pleasing confusion of titillation and tenderness. "That stung."

"Mhm," Selma agreed, fascinated by how rapidly the grease set again, creating a white, uneven blob over Edith's freckled skin. "This is just a little foretaste, my dear. What is really going to sting is when I rip it off you, pulling at all those sweet, babyish fuzzy hairs of yours. Now read. That was a rather grotesque first sentence, by the way. I hope we'll get into the good stuff soon."

Out of the corner of her eye, Selma noticed that Edith paled a little at the critique. She knew very well her companion-in-life was touchy about her writing, and she had never insisted on being shown a first draft. She had to tread carefully. But damn it, she also knew the potential for that hurt to transcend into a deliciously passionate lovemaking session. Edith relished a good critique. Almost, if not quite, as much as a harsh fuck. Suddenly hot in her clothes, Selma undid the top buttons of her blouse, purposely swaying the candle so that random drops of wax mottled the sprawled-out body on the desk.

"Read."

Edith read. Selma listened dreamily, all the while creating her own little pattern of pain with each bead of grease falling over that tender spine.

"Miss Selima would be back from the dance in a matter of moments, and her bedroom was in a right state. Edna went hot and cold with the rising panic, ineffectually gathering up gowns and fitting them onto hangers with trembling fingers, the silky fabric slipping from her grip more often than not."

Selma twisted her fingers in Edith's hair. Her head rose up a little further, the tendons in her neck bulging.

"Did they have hangers in those days?"

"I... I would have thought." Edith looked flustered. Arched into a perverse half-cobra pose like this, her breasts swayed tantalizingly, just centimeters from the table top. Selma fought the urge to throw the candle away and start squeezing them like a madwoman.

"Do your research," she chided, dropping another fat dollop of grease at the high end of Edith's lumbar spine. Edith made that wonderful throaty noise again. "I like the names."

"Edna's fear was palpable," Edith continued, her confidence growing. "Her mistress took a wicked delight in reporting any transgressions among the servants to her father, who summarily enforced his reprimands by way of a cane. He was a cruel old ogre, a remnant of an age gone by."

Selma blew out the candle. She needed some of it left.

"A cane, hmm? You need to flesh that out. You're doing too much telling, not enough showing. Here...", she added generously, reaching into the bottom drawer to fetch a broad, black belt. "I'll help you get in the mood."

She delivered two quick cracks across Edith's exposed behind, making her all but scramble up the table. She pulled, automatically, on the straps. Some stray pearls of candle wax loosened and fell from her side.

"Bad girl, you're ruining my artwork here. Stand still, will you?" Selma stroked the hot arse, changing the tone of Edith's moan from pain to rapture again. She pushed into the table, her behind lifting a little to give Selma a full view of her shimmering labial lips, fat and swollen with need. Selma's insides wrenched. She was reeling on her feet. Steadying herself against the corner of the desk with her left hand, she grabbed the belt to dole out a series of pathetically feeble blows with her right. The sheer number had the desired effect, though. Edith grunted, broke into a sweat, but, as she was told, stood still.

"Ed…" Selma muttered, letting the belt thud to the floor as her fingers feathered and fanned over that red-and-white derrière again. "For fuck's sake, read."

She stroked and slapped playfully with soft palms as she tried to listen to the turn of events. Predictably, her lady-in-waiting's willful oversight awoke the supreme miss Selima's ire. But to Edna's consternation, the lady did not ring for her father. Instead…

*'Lie on the bed,' Miss Selima ordered imperiously. Edna felt an unnerving flutter in her constricted chest. True, it would not be the first time she lay among her mistress's sheets, but that was a secret pleasure, hid, in part, even from herself. She had certainly never dreamt of doing such a thing with Selima present in the room.*

*'Lie on the bed,' Selima purred. 'Or I will call for my father.'*

*Edna hastened over to the large four-poster behemoth, filled to the brim with the softest linen. A queer but exquisite sensation rippled through her, as so often when she was ordered about by her fair superior. She hurriedly removed her coarse boots and lay on top of the duvet, hands clasped on her stomach.*

*'You are lying as though you are awaiting your lover,'* Selima *noted, amused. 'Do you often receive brutes in my bed?'*

*Edna felt the blood rush to her cheeks. 'No, Miss. Indeed not, Miss.'*

*'No?' Selima spun her hand in an elegant circle in the air, motioning for the maid to lie on her belly. 'I would have imagined you servant girls had all had your cherry picked and plundered before you reached the age of thirteen. Are you sincerely telling me you still have your maidenhead intact?'*

*Edna lay silent against her mistress's eiderdown pillows. She was not sure how to respond. What would upset the capricious woman the least?*

*'Tell me the truth, little Edna,' Selima offered, her tone soft and conciliatory, honey to heal the bee's sting. Even as she uttered the words, Edna could feel something pulling at her left foot. She turned around to see her mistress tying one of her silk shawls around her ankle, fastening it to the wooden post. Her heartbeat raced.*

*'I am a virgin,' she replied, praying that the truth would set her free. Selima tied up the other ankle, then went on to treat her wrists the same. Edna tugged surreptitiously at her bonds. They wouldn't budge. She was well and truly trapped. Selima came up to the head of the bed, so that she could look the servant girl in the eyes. A cruel smile played on her lips as she brandished one of her father's canes, pilfered from his study for this singular opportunity.*

*'Well, well, are you now? I am afraid I shan't believe you until I have the proof of it on my own fair hands.'*

Selma ran her hand up Edith's back, interrupting the mesmerizing voice with hundreds of tiny stings as fat blobs of candle wax came loose. Edith's body shook, she panted and bucked against the table. Selma fell over her, grinding her own throbbing want against her, her hands going under to pull at Edith's breasts.

"Ah," Edith went into the half-cobra again, of her own accord. Selma squeezed and stroked, pushing her excited limbs against the woman she had strapped to the desk. Ed nuzzled her behind into her, as well as she could, her own need leaking down her thighs. Selma reached for the abandoned candle stump, teasing it just inside Edith's ravenous vulva, the nubbly ends scraping the delicate walls.

"Oh God," Edith whimpered, trying to push back over it, but Selma held a steady hand over her tailbone, her own breath coming in heavy, uneven gusts.

"This is delicious," Selma said, running the candle along Edith's labia, pushing at the lowermost end of her back until she lay flat and limp against the desk, babbling softly with held-back ecstasy. "I do feel like vicariously ravaging a virgin tonight. You have included that bit, haven't you?"

Edith nodded weakly.

"Good, good. I'd hate for you to have to make it up on the fly. Like that time in Greece, remember? So easily distracted." Without warning, Selma pushed the candle deep and fully into her. Edith cried out.

"Such a naughty girl," Selma tsked, spreading Edith's legs still wider apart. "Here you are, ignobly strapped to your desk, reading out your smut while I do my best to teach you a lesson about duties and obligations, and what happens? You end up begging me for it, don't you? Getting turned on by your own purple passages? What do you say?"

"Please," Edith groaned, shaking from the strain of keeping her balance with her legs spread at a forty-five degree angle.

"Please what?" Selma insisted, keeping the candle quite still in Edith's softly contracting cunt. She dug her nails into the tender flesh of her groin to keep her from coming too soon.

"Please fuck me, please. I'm dying here."

"Not so fast, Lady Lazarus. All right, I will, since you ask nicely. And you will read me that enticing last page. Tell me how Selima plucks that ripe little peach of hers. Might give me ideas."

Slowly, inexorably, Selma began sliding the candle stump in and out of Edith. She was careful not to touch any other part of her, keeping the rhythm to a mere snail's pace. Tears of frustration glinted at the corners of Edith's eyes as she propped herself up again to be able to decipher her own handwriting.

*The sensitive skin of Edna's bottom had turned a strawberry shade of pink from Selima's ministrations with the cane. She was splayed out, tied to the bedposts with her mistress's silk, weeping bitterly. Even her private parts wept. There was a strange humming glow at the pit of her stomach for which she could not account. She did not feel ill, exactly, she felt…*

*She felt her lady's hands stroking her sore bum, pushing her dress up further along her back and plunging between her legs to catch the moistness of her secret place.*

*'Oh dear,' Selima lisped, a strange note of tenderness to her voice. 'What is this now?'*

*'I…' Edna was at a loss for words. She blushed deeply, and yet some animal instinct, one she had only indulged once or twice before, alone, in this very bed, made her press against the hand fondling her.*

*'Hmm.' Selima pushed back, up, until Edna found herself positioned on her hands and knees. 'I think we are done with your correction for tonight. Now for my prize…'*

*Incredulous, Edna watched through her arms as the lady placed herself between her naked thighs. There was nothing she could do to stop the sticky liquid from dripping down upon that regal face. Selima caught some stray drops of it on her cheek with her finger, then put the finger in her mouth.*

*'Yes,' she sighed. 'This will be a treat.'*

*She bent her head backwards to look up at Edna. Their eyes met. Selima smiled. A cryptic, lop-sided expression.*

*'You could have cried out, Edna. This is not the Middle Ages. Someone would have come.'*

*The words, the earnest gaze, jolted the servant-girl. They were thick with meaning, laced with an odd message about her rights, free choice, and love. She was tied up, her behind still aching from the corporal punishment, yet she had never felt so liberated. If she did cry out, if she did bring rescuers to the door, Selima would be shamed for life. Perhaps even sent away to some mental asylum, where a delicate constitution like hers could not last long. This was the power proffered to her. Her mistress's very life prostrated before her.*

*Edna shook her head.*

*'No, ma'am,' she whispered.*

*Selima nodded.*

*'I am going to deflower you now, sweet servant of mine. You can watch, if you like.'*

"Oh fuuuuuck…" Edith's voice broke as the tip of Selma's tongue flicked her clit.

"Geez," Selma murmured derisively from her crouching position between the poor writer's violently trembling legs, back snug up against the hardwood side of the desk. "Did I interrupt? I do apologize. Only all this reading you're doing, brilliantly, may I add, is getting me so hot and bothered. I really don't think I can listen to another sentence without eating you out. You don't mind, do you? A short break?"

"That's… oooh."

Selma really had no time to wait for a verbal response. Her lover was thick, lush and ready for her, an over-ripe plum beckoning for her attention. She dove in and gluttonously sucked all the juicy bits into her mouth at once. Edith convulsed. Selma suckled harder, pushing the fingers of her right hand into Edith's wide-open cunt, rubbing along that lovely inch with her left to find the tighter crack behind. Aided by Ed's own profusions, she slid her slick index and middle fingers up her anus. The snug bud closed around them and she was instantly rewarded by a sweet and salty fountain from the front, spurting over her face and neck, running down her cleavage like a humid rainfall. Selma felt her own orgasm erupting uncontrollably; hurriedly, she drew her right hand from Edith and put it up under her own skirt, teasing herself to a proper one while her tongue still leisurely lapped up the flow from Edith's mushy parts.

She could swear she saw asterisks.

* * *

"Sel... Are you still there?"

Edith nudged her wife's lax body as gently as she could with her all but numb right foot. As she moved it, pins and needles were shooting up like sparks from her sole and straight up to her hip. She grimaced to herself. Concerned at the lack of a reply, she expertly released herself from the straps. Massaging her chafed wrists, she pushed herself up from the table. Selma sat huddled against the desk, eyes closed, an expression of sheer bliss across her sleeping face. Her clothes were in wild disarray. Edith noted that her knee-length skirt was pulled up to her hips, her knickers halfway down her thighs. Her right hand still rested over her pudenda. She pulled on her cardigan, never mind the rest, and kneeled to lift the drowsing damsel off the floor. She glanced over at the unfinished story spread out on the music stand. It could wait until tomorrow.

As she started on the second flight of stairs to their upstairs apartment, Selma awoke briefly. She snuggled in closer to her chest, fingering the half-open cardigan.

"You know," she said sleepily, "that was not a bad story. Great potential."

"Mmm," Edith agreed, reaching the top of the stairs and angling her burden over a little to the side so that she could push the bedroom door open.

"What are you writing next?"

Edith arched her brows. "I haven't even finished this one yet."

She threw the giggling imp onto the bed, cast her specs and cardigan to the side and crashed down beside her, pulling the cover up over them.

"I've still got my clothes on," Selma protested.

"Have you now?"

"Oh, you're incorrigible!"

Selma slipped from Edith's roving hands to help herself out of the blouse and bra. She unbuttoned her skirt and let it fall to the floor, obviously taken aback to be standing in all her naked glory all of a sudden.

"Where are my underpants?"

Edith shrugged, holding the cover up for Selma to get into bed again.

"You're a thief, too. Now tell me." Selma grudgingly crawled back into her waiting embrace.

"Witches, I think," Edith mused, letting Selma arrange them into her favorite joint sleeping position. "Something about witches."

"Yes," Sel enthused, "herbs, and mortars, and brews. I could work with that."

Edith put her nose in Selma's mussed hair, savoring the scent of faint postcoital perspiration.

"I wonder what will happen to Edna and Selima though. Is there really any chance for them? Will they live happily ever after?"

"Realistically speaking…" Edith checked herself as her bedmate frowned up at her. She let her hand glide down to Selma's full, round hip, caressing it with long and steadfast strokes. "Relax," she mumbled, "I'm sure they live perversely ever after."

Selma turned in her arms, all but crushing Edith with her generous bosom.

"Perversely ever after. Now that I can seriously work with."

# TELL ME
## ROBYN NYX

**Friday 9:03 p.m.**

"Tell me."

"I can't."

"Please. I want to know."

"You'll judge me. It's too dark."

"I like dark."

* * *

**Saturday 11:38 a.m.**

"How can I ever truly know you if you don't tell me these things?"

"Maybe you won't want to know me if I *do* tell you these things."

"This is how we started, baby. We wouldn't be together right now if we hadn't been honest with each other."

"I don't know, babe. Some things are just meant to stay fantasies."

"Are they? Why?"

* * *

**Saturday 7:14 p.m.**

"I'm never gonna leave it. I want to know everything that turns you on. Everything."

"Even if I told you, it's not something we could do anyway, so there's no point."

"Why couldn't we do it?"

"Because…"

"It involves more than two people?"

"Maybe…"

"C'mon, baby, just tell me."

* * *

**Sunday 1:23 a.m.**

"You know how we don't have friends yet?"

"Because all of our old friends chose unwisely in the divorce?"

Giggles.

"Their loss, yes. But anyway, I've kind of got other friends…"

"Meaning?"

"Friends who like to play the games we do."

Shy laughter.

* * *

**Sunday 4:36 a.m.**

"Baby, are you awake?"

"I am. You've finally come around?"

Deep sigh.

"I love when you beat me like that, I love when you raise my tattoo with the belt. It makes me feel so connected to you."

"I was born to be your Master, babe. I've been waiting for you my whole life."

Heavy silence.

"Please tell me your go-to scenario."

"If I instruct you as your Master to leave this alone, will you?"

"I don't think I can, no."

* * *

**Sunday 10:17 a.m.**

"I can do that. Let me make it happen."

"I don't think so, babe. I don't know if I could handle other people being involved with this, with us."

"It won't change anything, I promise."

"I know that. We're titanium. But, still… I think this fantasy should stay just that. I think you should just forget it."

"I don't wanna."

Pouty face.

* * *

### Three weeks later, Friday 1:08 p.m.

"I know I've already told you this is my favourite city in the world, but I have to tell you again. I fucking love this place."

"It *is* beautiful, babe, you're absolutely right. There's nothing quite like being in a place you've seen so often in the movies. There's a kind of twisted reality to it."

"The perfect location for our playtime, yeah?"

"You're still okay to go ahead with that?"

"Baby, as wonderful as Venice is, I brought you here to fulfil your fantasy and that's what we're gonna do."

"I'm just saying, it wouldn't matter if we didn't. It's enough that you listened and didn't baulk. Thank you for that."

"I want to. And I mean, I really want to. I can't wait for tomorrow night."

* * *

### Saturday 10:55 p.m., Calle de la Passion

*So, I guess this is it.* I look up at the old street sign, the peeling plaster and the mismatched bricks in the wall. It's in stark contrast to the adjacent, orange bricked, pristine tower. The lamp with its fancy cast-iron bracket seems out of place, stuck as it is to the crumbling bricks, but it lends a certain extra beauty to the dilapidated building. I spent the last fifteen minutes staring into the windows of a handmade paper shop because I arrived too early, misjudging how long it would take me to get here. This city is a maze of tiny Shakespearean-type alleyways, barely wide enough for two people to pass each other without getting a little intimate and a lot lost. I can practically see Desdemona and Othello making out down the narrow passage in which I now stand. The Carnival is in full swing and I feel slightly out of place in my jeans and leather jacket. I'd been far more appropriately dressed last night at the 'Grand Feast of the Gods' at the Palazzo Flangini. My love dressed as Venus, and I as Bacchus. I close my eyes and picture her before me now, in her flowing white silk dress, a necklace of seashells, and her crown of myrtle flowers. I connect with the deep throbbing between my legs, and recall the image of her on her knees in our hotel room, as my rose petal cat-o'-nine tails lashed over her back. Me, working her back with wanton need. Her, moaning with sated lust at each stroke.

The tower bells begin to chime and I slip back into the moment.

Time to start running. I pull the straps of my backpack tight and head down Passion Lane, a wildly apposite place to begin this particular journey.

\* \* \*

Dead ends. Canal offshoots too wide to jump and no bridge to cross them. As I've ventured further away from the *turista* areas, the proliferation of people has diminished and the streetlights are few. But I'm getting close and my heart is pounding. What's about to happen, various iterations of it, has been the stuff of my wank-bank since my formative years, when I discovered the happy correlation between the warm feeling in my pants and someone putting a beating on someone else. I turn the final corner to this fantasy-come-reality, and see her. She's leaning against the stone wall and looking right at me. She smiles that beautiful smile that captured me months ago, and it steels my resolve. I trust her. Implicitly. *Let's do this.*

"Are you lost, handsome?" She has a perfect Italian accent.

"I am, yeah, but I wouldn't want to trouble you. I hear the average Venetian is asked for directions so many times a day, all they end up saying is 'straight on'... uh, *sempre dritto.* I've heard it a lot today."

"Getting lost is the most magical way to discover Venice, my English friend, but it's getting late and the *vaporetto* doesn't run for too much longer. Where are you going?"

I hear footsteps and spin around to see who's coming. A couple look up the alley, and see it's a dead end. They turn on their heels and are gone, the girl giggling as they disappear from sight. I turn back. "Anywhere. I'm going anywhere."

She raises her eyebrow and tilts her head slightly. "Are you going somewhere, or getting away from someone?"

I smile at her. She is *so* beautiful. Her long, blonde hair reaches all the way down to her waist. Her blue eyes sparkle and they make me simultaneously weak with lust, and strong with desire. She's diminutive, and I note the steel wrapped heels of New Rock boots which raise her stature. She's still a few inches shorter than me so I can enjoy looking down at her. "I'm just adventuring, lady, I don't mind where I end up."

"There's a rough wind coming in from the Adriatic, our *acqua alta* is unusually high right now. If you don't get off the lagoon soon, you will have to find someone to amuse yourself with for an hour or two."

"Are you offering?"

"My services come at a high price, handsome, and you

don't seem like someone who needs to pay for it. Unless you're looking for something very specific." She moves in, and slips her hands inside my jacket. They feel like hot acid searing through the thin fabric of my t-shirt. "I think you would like to see me on my knees, taking your cock in my mouth, no?" One hand is now on the crotch of my jeans, firmly rubbing at my clit, which is responding and hardening with every caress. "I think you would like my lips on your boots." Her other hand steadily traces my shoulder muscles. "And your belt across my back."

"That may be so, lovely lady, and you are a fine example of female perfection, but I still don't pay for it."

She pulls away and it's all I can do to stop my body lurching forward to pin her to the wall. I want to wrap my hand around her throat, thrust my fingers between her legs and feel how wet she is. Teasing me this way will have her soaking, I know this. I can practically smell it on her. She reeks of our desire for each other.

"And you are quite the specimen, too. You're in fine, fine shape. Like the Mercury statue at *Palazzo Ducale*, you feel like you are carved from stone."

Physically and psychologically, she knows exactly how to stroke me. "Alas, it's not for you, beautiful lady." A heartbeat of a pause. "Unless you're inclined to take a break for a while? This doesn't look like a particularly busy part of the city for you to be pedalling your wares for passing trade."

She flashes her flawless teeth in a wide smile, and there's that look in her eye when she's desperate, absolutely desperate to have my hands on her.

"I suppose it will be a while before the grand balls open their doors to let their players out for the night."

She touches my cheek. My jaw's clenched, as it is when I'm mad with either desire or anger. She knows which it is.

"Follow me, my love."

She turns away and I smile at her slip of the tongue. *I'll follow you to the ends of the earth.* I watch her quickly tap something on her mobile phone. It must be something to do with her 'friends'. Though I've given her a vague outline of my darkest fantasy, I've no clear idea what lies ahead.

* * *

"I have the ideal tool for you, *bello*. I am sure you will like." She opens one of the heavy drawers in the antique-looking cupboard beside what may be the biggest bed I've ever seen. From it, she pulls out a hefty looking leather cat o' nine tails and drops it on the sheets. She dips back in and retrieves a thick leather harness, already coupled with an eight-inch behemoth of a dildo in black, marbled silicone. She holds it aloft for inspection.

"You look far too petite to take something like that comfortably." *I know I wouldn't let that thing anywhere near me.*

"I'm not so fond of being comfortable, handsome." She's got it fixed on my hips in no time, and she stands back, admiring it against my black clad legs. I begin to shrug off my jacket, but she puts her hand on my shoulder and stops me. "Leave it on."

I grasp her wrist tightly and force her to her knees. It doesn't take much effort, she's eager to be down there.

"Suck me off, pretty lady."

She wraps her delicate hands around the base of the shaft and she looks at me as her tongue passes over the tip of my new cock. She's so good at this, she makes it feel like it's actually part of me. She runs her tongue from its tip down to her hands on both sides, teasing me, daring me to lose patience with her. All the while, her blue eyes are focused on mine, enjoying my reaction. I slip my hand around the back of her head and ball my fist in her soft hair. She gasps around my cock and I can see in her eyes that small action has travelled directly to her pussy. I force the dildo deeper into her mouth and she starts to choke on it. Her hands release and push against my hips, trying to stop herself from gagging, but it's no use. I'm stronger. I'll always be stronger. Her eyes widen and tear up as I shove my hips toward her face, using her exactly the way we both love.

I pull her to her feet and propel her toward the bare stone wall. Her breath escapes her involuntarily as she smashes against it. I push her skirt up over her waist and let out my own involuntary breath as I see she's wearing no panties. I pick her up and she wraps her legs around my waist, taking my massive cock easily, crying out and swearing at me in Italian. I slap her hard, and drowsy desire swamps her eyes again.

"Don't swear at me, lady." Each word is punctuated with a hefty thrust of my hips, powering my thick dildo inside her.

She's switching between yelling "*Sì*" and "Yes", and combining it with "*non cazzo arresto*" which, with my pigeon Italian, I know roughly translates as "Don't you dare fucking stop what you're doing."

She comes, hard and loud, her body spasming violently and I struggle to hold onto her. I press her harder to the wall and wait it out, my teeth fixed against her neck as my groaning matches hers. I love the way she comes for me. No one's ever fucked her this hard, she's told me. I wonder why. She screamed for me to use her this harshly without the words ever passing her lips. Neglectful lovers.

We transfer to the bed and I flip her over onto her hands and knees. She opens her knees wide, and I push back in. She howls into the duvet, but takes me all the way up to the harness with barely a pause. I pick up the cat she'd nonchalantly dropped onto the bed earlier and bring it down across her shoulders. This kind of thing takes rhythm and timing: a thrust of the hips, a lash of the cat. But the result is worth the effort. She opens up for me deeper, and she's moaning, calling out for God and begging me never to stop doing this. *Not fucking likely, sweet slave of mine. I'll own you forever.*

And in that most perfect moment, as she pushes back against me and screams out another body-jerking orgasm, the door swings open and four extremely good-looking ruffians burst in.

* * *

"What took you so long?" No longer does she seem impressed by my rhythmic cockmanship. Now, still with her pussy on show for all to see, she sits regally yet rudely, castigating the interlopers for not interrupting sooner.

I've been hauled off her, stripped of my most excellent endowment and am pinned against one of the old wooden posts suspending the ceiling by two of the intruders.

"Our sincere apologies, Mistress, no excuses will suffice."

I like her turn of phrase, and decide I'll call her Shay, short for Shakespeare. Though she doesn't know it, it's a high honour indeed.

"You disappoint me." Her tone is all hues of black promise.

*Oh, now here's a talent that lay undiscovered, babe.*

Shay turns to me and takes the reprimand out on my stomach with her fist. "Allow us to make it up to you, Mistress."

I was tense and ready for it. She didn't get the response she wanted, so she hits me again, before her palm connects with my face and hammers my head against the post. I see a smattering of stars.

"Lanza." She addresses the fourth stranger tersely.

"Yes, Mistress." Lanza steps forward and bows her head.

I'm amused to see someone submit to the woman who kneels for me, but I have to concede she seems to possess a natural talent for this particular position.

"Come to me, on your knees." Lanza does as

instructed, and crawls faultlessly to her Mistress. She pulls Lanza's head between her legs and closes her eyes for a moment as the woman's tongue connects with her clit. She looks at Shay with hard, indecent eyes. "So make it up to me."

Shay nods and turns to me. "Who the fuck do you think you are, you English punk? Treating our Mistress as you have? Pretending to be a Master—when you're clearly a boi."

*Ah, there it is. The word that has the power to melt me.* Everyone in the room sees it in my eyes. The ones holding me must surely feel me soften in their grip.

"Now you get to find out what our Mistress lets us do to bois like you."

Shay nods to the two holding me and I'm shoved to my knees. She unzips her jeans and pulls out a dildo. I'm thankful it's nowhere near the size I used earlier.

"Fuck if you think you're sticking that thing in my mouth."

She laughs and I can feel the sharp tip of a knife under my chin. In my peripheral vision, I see the Mistress' eyes fixed on me while Lanza does her best to service her. *Am I going to be jealous when she makes her come?*

Shay slaps me hard to bring my attention back to her and the dildo she's proudly produced.

"I'll cut your mouth open if you don't let me in willingly."

Shay's got an aggressive energy about her that makes me think that, although right now we're playing, maybe she's done that to someone before me. I hesitate and she presses the knifepoint a little harder. My lips part, she grabs my chin and rams her cock into my mouth. I choke, and try to pull away, but my head hits the wooden post again, and I feel a little dizzy. I can't breathe around it, and saliva's oozing unattractively out of the corners of my mouth as my tongue struggles to make room for the brutish face-fucking she's forcing on me.

I can still see her, with Lanza stationed between her legs, and she's smiling cruelly, clearly enjoying the show. I wonder if she'll ever be able to look at me the same again. *Will this change how you view your Master? This wasn't what you signed up for when you put pen to paper on our contract.*

Shay pulls out and I'm hauled to my feet. She puts her left hand on my shoulder, and digs her thumb hard into my collarbone. She pounds her right fist into my gut, giving me just enough time to inhale and tense before each blow forces the breath right out of me. I count ten before my head's hanging just a little and I'm hoping for a break.

"Enough. Bring her to me."

Shay looks a tad disappointed, but releases her grip and the two others drag me over to the bed.

She pushes Lanza away, seizes a fistful of my hair and draws me close to the intoxicating smell of her delicious cunt. "Do you want to taste me… boi?"

I'm instantly a mess. To hear Shay say it was hot enough, but for her… is she *my* Mistress now? For the word to emanate from her mouth, in that slow, seductive and certain tone, that's just not fair. *Don't answer.* If I allow myself to speak, I'll be at her feet, worshipping the ornately stencilled leather boots I so admired earlier this evening.

She slaps me and my head snaps to the side. She's got a solid hit for such a delicate frame.

"If you're reluctant to serve me, boi, I'll just have to beat you until you *drop* to your knees." She caresses my face before slapping me again. "Strip her down."

I flash a warning look at her. We discussed this. I like to be beaten with my clothes on. I'm not that kind of pain-whore. Her hand fixes around my throat as she sees my attempt to communicate with her.

"You're not paying for this, so you don't get to tell me what to do."

Another firm slap before my jacket's pulled from me

and my t-shirt is torn off. Her mouth opens slightly. Despite being in role, she can't help it. She loves my body. She's always wanted a muscular woman, and never had one. I'm being pulled around and everything is strained as I writhe in my captor's clutches. Most of it, I'm just tensing for show to please her. "String her up."

Whoever these friends are, they know what they're doing with rope. I'm tied facing the same wooden post, my hands pulled high and fastened tight. My feet are just touching the floor. I feel her breath on the back of my neck and her warm, familiar touch on my hips. She bites down hard and I pointlessly try to squirm away, even though I know there's nowhere to go. Even though there's nowhere I want to go.

"You can scream, boi. No one will hear you through these old stone walls."

"You won't hear me screaming, lady."

She laughs softly against my shoulders. "You will scream for me, boi. I guarantee it."

Her voice and the words she speaks send a chill up my spine. "No one's made me scream before."

She whispers into my ear so her friends can't hear, "No one had made you come from fucking you before, but that happened."

I can't resist a smile. The lady has a point. There's been lots of 'never befores' in the past half year.

She moves away and I miss her instantly. The first strike of the cat surprises me and pitches me forward. She doesn't pace them, just delivers swing after swing that assaults my bare back, and sends me higher than I've ever been on drugs in my twenties. The cat thuds into my muscles and nestles there comfortably, before she strips it away only to bring it down again. I'm oblivious to anything else in the room now. Could be, my lady's friends have left already. Nothing else exists, nothing but the exacting embrace of the leather around my body, wielded so expertly by my novice

Mistress. Some things you just can't teach, some things are simply natural talents.

I count 129 before she stops. I know she's high like me, high from the power she feels in her hands, hot from watching how my skin reddens and welts under her labours. As the lashes hit, I heard the lusty breaths escape from her mouth. I've recently discovered there's nothing on earth like it, the first time you beat the one you love. Not just a bottom, not merely a submissive or a slave for the night, or the length of a contract, but the one you can see forever with. The one who *really sees* you, all your dark and your light, and embraces it. Welcomes it. Reflects you like a mirror.

"Turn her around."

Her friends must still be here. And I don't fight now. The fight has left the building on the tail of the hot air currents produced from my Mistress's whip. I can stand but my body feels incorporeal, and yet so deeply and viscerally connected to my mind. She's done that for me. No one's ever done that for me.

My hands are secured above my head, my chest and stomach muscles pulled taut. Her hands caress me, follow the curves and rips. I ache to feel her inside me, but I can see she's not sated. She's nowhere near done with that whip. I know that yearning, it lives and breathes inside me every day.

"Look at me."

*Oh God, there's nowhere I'd rather look, babe.* That's the look I've been searching my entire existence for. It's the same look I know is in my eyes when I beat her. And those light blue eyes, accented as they are with black liner, scream sex at me, and promise the wild, obscene intimacy I've craved my whole life. I don't think I can adequately verbalise how weightless she makes me feel when she looks at me that way.

She starts again with the whip, and I know immediately that it won't be long before she draws the scream she demands. The beatings I've had in the past have been concentrated on my back, *con* clothes. I've never been beaten naked before, and never on my breasts. *Is this what being scared feels like?* Am I scared I can't take what she has to give? Will she be disappointed in me if I can't? Will she think less of me as her Master?

The lashes pull me back into the room, back to her, back to her eyes. We connect the way we do when *I* bring us to the core, the truth of what we are together, as Master and slave. It was risky disclosing this fantasy to her, it could change everything, but she can't fake that look in her eyes. She's discovering something within herself she never knew existed. I can tell she's a little unsure about what she's doing, but she's obviously enjoying herself nonetheless.

Every lash is a stroke of profound, unconditional love and they rip right through me, tearing the screams from my lungs. She's smiling, all smug and self-satisfied that she got what she wanted, something I'd never given anyone else. We came together in our fourth decade on this planet, when the 'firsts' are not as exciting as they were in our twenties. The first cervical screening. The first cholesterol test. The first time someone in their twenties tells you they see you as their mom instead of their sister, or a potential love interest. We've had the first kiss, the first fuck, the first 'I love you.' It's a time of my life when I thought there was nothing I could say that I hadn't said before. But I was so wrong. This is a new forever, with plenty of firsts. And here we are, in my first multi-player situation as a boi, and I'm screaming for my Mistress. Another first.

Her lips are on mine and it's my lover's kiss, but it's rougher, harder, dominant. She forces her tongue inside my mouth. It's a violent violation, and it takes my breath away. She's never kissed me like this before, with such a power-soaked intensity. She drapes the cat around my neck and pulls me closer.

"What were you saying about your screams, boi?" There's a self-congratulatory tone in her voice that's so damn sexy. I try to look away but she takes hold of my chin and makes me face her. "You are like the *Cascate del Serio* down here, are you not?" Her other hand presses against my hot mess of a pussy through my jeans.

*Yeah, you're right. You've made me soak like a waterfall down there.*

"Women like you are all the same, always in control and yet, secretly wanting to be controlled, taken *against* their will, subjugated."

She unbuckles my belt and her graceful hands open my jeans, seductively slowly, and I can't help but watch. She knows I love to watch her undress me. I love to observe her delicately handling me. She nods to the side and there are other hands on me. My boots and jeans are discarded.

She comments on my lack of underwear. "Filthy whore."

Shay and Lanza pull my legs wide apart, straining my body from my bound wrists, and I can feel their hot breath close to my sodden lips. She presses her fingers to my vulnerable and completely exposed hole and laughs as she slips three inside me a little too easily for me to look convincingly affronted and abused. I look down as she pulls out, and sticks her fingers into Lanza's open, waiting mouth. Her other hand fills me, before pulling out and doing the same to Shay. She keeps her eyes fixed on me while she fucks their faces with a mix of her hands and my slick juices.

I'm desperate for her to be back inside me, and she knows it. She loves fucking me, another first for her, pillow queen that she used to be. She's like a kid in a candy store, a very grown-up kid, playing grown-up games, in a filthy candy store for deviants. *I know* she won't be able to resist much longer. I think she can see my arrogance and maybe she considers denying me for a moment. But it's a fleeting moment, one of those 'cut your nose off to spite your face' kind of thoughts that don't last all that long. She's back and fucking me hard, crushing my body between her and the unforgiving wooden post. Her hand doesn't feel quite so small now it's inside me, and she's straight into the rhythm that we recently discovered makes me come like a fire hose. Yeah, another first. She's got me swearing and grinding down on her hand unashamedly. Fuck the scene right now, my body has no choice but to respond to her. Her other hand fists in my hair and drives my head back against the post. Her mouth is all over me, nibbling and biting at my breasts, my abs, my shoulders. I mark easily and the more she sees that, the more she wants to see. She's acting like a wolf marking her territory, and I'm glad she's using her teeth. I can feel there are other tongues, teeth and hands on my lower body, but they barely register. It almost feels like she owns them all and she's all over me. No one else figures.

"Come for me, boi."

*I wouldn't have asked for permission. I'm not that kind of boi.* And yet, her words, her voice, add the extra that's been missing in the years before her, though those memories are fading fast and it already feels like we've been together for years.

My orgasm escapes me in a rush of curses and come. I thrash in my bondage with the welcome release. She holds me tight to her as my body submits entirely to her will. Slowly, she pulls her hand from me and I can hear Shay savouring her Mistress's hard earned prize.

My Mistress's cohorts carefully take me down from the post, carry me to the bed, lay me down, and drape a silk blanket over my body. I hear the door open and close, and know we're finally alone.

My lover crawls under the blanket and snuggles in beside me.

"Tell me another one…"

# TAKING THE LEAD
## LAUREN JADE

I stood at the vanity in our bathroom and rolled the snug, slinky fabric of my dress down over my hips and adjusted the hem to lay right above my knees. The dress was Steph's favorite—sleek, low cut, and jet-black. Turning to check my profile in the mirror, I admired how the dress hugged my curves and pushed my breasts up and together, making them look a good cup size larger than they actually were. Some call it false advertisement. I call it being ingenious. My silhouette was smooth—nothing out of the ordinary to see here. I adjusted the silicone cock that was pressed against my inner thigh under my smoothing, suck-it-in, no-panty-line underwear. After swiping on a fiery red lipstick my mother would not have approved of, I gave my long black hair one last brush, flipped off the bathroom light, and closed the door behind me.

Trotting down the stairs, black stilettos in hand, I saw Steph standing in front of our large foyer mirror adjusting her bowtie. We'd been together almost four years—since just after I graduated from college. I still couldn't control my smirk and the flurry of butterflies in my stomach when I saw her. She turned to face me when my weight made the floorboards squeak, running her hand through her short blonde hair.

"You look nice," I said, smiling and sitting down on the bottom step to strap on my shoes, careful not to let my dress ride up and reveal what else I was strapping on. She was incredibly handsome. In a white button-down dress shirt, grey slacks, and dusty blue suspenders and bowtie she was the sexy tomboy that I knew could always make me go weak in the knees. Her sleeves were rolled up to the elbows, revealing the bottom portion of the colorful Japanese-themed tattoo sleeve on her left arm. She tucked her hands into her pockets, and I wondered if she did it on purpose because as she stretched the fabric over her pelvis, I noticed a faint bulge. She was packing as well. I felt my face flame and turned my focus to the buckle of my shoe. I could have sworn I caught her grin out of the corner of my eye.

I stood, smoothing my dress back down over my thighs.

"I love this dress on you," she said, smirking and swaggering over to me. She grabbed my waist in her hands and slid them down over my hips.

"I know," I quipped, running my pointer finger up and down underneath one of her suspenders.

She grabbed my wrist and pinned it behind my back, leaning in close to me. "I love it more when it's on the ground," she whispered. Her hot breath on my neck shot a tingle down my spine. Her other hand moved from my hip across my thigh. I quickly grabbed it and put it back by her side, safely away from my secret. She took a step back looking shocked, eyed me and released my wrist.

I was abruptly nervous. She could take me right then for batting her hand away, and I knew I would let her. I wanted to keep this secret I wore under my dress, and to see how this fantasy of mine was going to play out, but cat and mouse was not a game frequently acted out in our house. I bit my lip and played coy, brushing past her and picking up my black clutch from the entry table. "We wouldn't want to be late," I said in my best sultry voice.

Her cutting glance turned soft and she smirked at me, pulling the car keys from her pocket and walking toward me. "You'll regret that later," she growled as she ran her hand roughly across my ass. She opened the door and started down the stoop stairs, clicking the car unlocked.

I breathed a sigh of relief—my secret was safe for now —and I followed her out, locking the door behind me.

We were headed to a wedding. Our friends Alicia and Sam had been planning their elegant affair at a South Nashville music venue for more than a year. Even though Steph always asserted that she wasn't the marrying type, I could've sworn I saw her tear up just a little bit during the vows when she reached over to squeeze my hand.

"Marriage is both parties giving one hundred percent," the robed pastor was saying into a microphone. "It's an equal partnership of two people working together, neither one dominating the other."

"Unless you're into that," Steph whispered, glancing in my direction. I kept my eyes on the couple at the front, but my stomach did a somersault thinking about the relationship Steph and I had behind closed doors. Usually our sessions left my wrists raw and my ass striped pink. I got off on having my power taken from me, and Steph got off on putting me in my place. I shifted in my seat and crossed my legs, enjoying the pressure the dildo was putting on me.

The reception was dimly lit and smelled like cocktails. We sat at a round table with two other couples. Wedding food is never stellar, and I pushed my asparagus around my plate while I sipped a glass of white wine.

"Do you want another?" Steph asked as she stood up with her empty champagne flute to get a refill. Part of me wondered if I shouldn't have another. Would I need all my wits about me to pull off this reverse power-play fantasy?

I decided I would need liquid courage more. "Yes, please," I answered and smiled at her. She kissed me on top of the head and headed toward the bar, chatting with another friend. I swallowed the last sip and let the warmth radiate through my veins. Steph had just begun walking back toward our table when the DJ cranked the music up. People poured onto the dance floor. Steph caught my gaze and held out my beverage, beckoning me to come to her.

Steph spun me around and around the dance floor, leading the whole time of course. I tried not to slosh sauvignon blanc onto our feet. She kept turning me so I was backing up into her—I knew her game. She wanted me to feel that she was packing. I grinned, thinking of my own little secret.

After a third glass of wine, a bouquet toss, and at least four terrible line dances, I decided I should make my move while I had the courage. During a particularly close dance I slinked my hand down and grabbed at her waistband. She smirked. I slid my hand into her front pocket and nudged her cock. "I'm ready to go home," I whispered in her ear. She grabbed me by the wrist without saying a word and dragged me toward the exit. I teetered behind her, anticipation building in my stomach.

The car ride home was tense. My mind raced, as I doubted myself. Our relationship had conditioned me to receive gratefully, but not to give. Steph enjoyed being in control, and I enjoyed being tied down, gagged, and told what to do. We made a perfect team. But for months now, I'd been fantasizing about what her face would look like if I took her. I knew the sounds of her having her way with me. What sounds would she make if I licked, sucked, and thrusted how *I* wanted? The thought made heat throb between my legs. I reached across the console as we pulled into our driveway and grasped Steph's member.

She smacked my hand away hard. "You're getting too bold," she stated. "I'll have to beat that out of you." She stepped out of the car, heading up our sidewalk and into our house. I followed, trying to hide the smile creeping across my face.

Steph dropped the keys in a basket on our entry table and headed straight up the stairs. She looked down from the top and harshly shouted down at me to hurry up.

I tossed my bag onto the floor and grasped the handrail firmly. *You can do this,* I thought as I ascended the stairs.

Steph stood by the dresser in our room, hands in her

pockets. I felt a jolt of pleasure that shook my nervousness out and replaced it with want. I entered our room and pushed the door hard enough for it to close, letting my eyes cut to Steph, who was standing in front of me undoing her bowtie.

"What is it?" she asked, looking startled.

Not breaking my gaze, I crossed the room and pressed my lips to hers, hard and sudden. She pulled back and started to say something, but I wrapped my hands around her cheeks and brought her into me again. I felt her melt into my lips and her tongue met mine, shooting sparks to all my nerve endings.

She pulled away again and took a step back, resuming her cool and calm demeanor. Her arms wiggled their way out from under the suspenders and they fell to her sides. "Baby, if you want me to fuck you," she said firmly as she kicked her shoes off, "you know you have to ask for it." It was clear she wasn't going to give up her power easily.

Wine and long-hidden fantasy made courage swell up in me. "That's not what's happening tonight," I said in my most authoritative voice as I closed the distance she'd put between us. "I'm going to fuck you."

Steph's eyes widened and she tipped her head to the side. "I should take you over my knee for what a cocktease you've been all night long, and now you think you're going to call the shots? No ma'am. Take that dress off." She had undone her pants and her bulge was apparent under her boxer briefs.

"No," I said decisively, crossing my arms over my chest.

Steph's eyes glimmered; she obviously thought I was still playing the part of a tease. She shook her pants down and kicked them to the side before grabbing me around the waist and pulling me into her. "Then I'll do it, and you'll pay for your disobedience." She ran her hands over my ass, squeezing hard before crossing my thighs and running a hand up them between my legs.

Steph stopped abruptly when her hand reached my cock. "What is that?" she asked, leaning back to glare at me.

I grinned. "I told you," I said. "I'm fucking you tonight."

Before she could respond I had grabbed her by the shoulders and pushed her down onto our bed. She still looked stunned, so I used the opportunity to my advantage. We had a restraint system permanently attached to our bedframe, and I quickly reached for the velvet-lined cuffs, securing first one hand, then the other above her head. As I unbuttoned her shirt, I noticed the pink flush on her chest—a giveaway that she was secretly loving every second of this.

"Cas, I don't know what the hell you think you're doing, but—"

"Shut your mouth," I interrupted, cupping my hand over her lips. I spread her shirt open, revealing the tank top that she wore instead of a bra. Her nipples protruded from the tight fabric. "If you really don't want this, then tell me to stop," I said as I ran my thumb over one of the tight buds and climbed up to straddle her. I took my hand away from her mouth, and she responded with a smirk. "That's what I thought," I said.

I grabbed the hem of her snug undershirt and slid it up, revealing her perfectly scored abs. I vowed to never complain about her early workouts again. Her chest was small, but flawlessly shaped, with her pink nipples rising from her pale skin. I leaned down and peppered kisses in a trail under her left breast, then over to her right. I felt her ribs rise with a gasp as I landed one directly on the apex. Sitting back, I traced my fingers lightly across the top of her underwear that fit snugly on her hipbones. Latching my thumbs underneath the waistband, I slowly rolled it down until the top of the silicone cock was visible.

"You won't need this," I teased, as I pulled it out and flung it to the floor. The expression on her face was one of shock, and possibly a little embarrassment. I'd successfully emasculated her. I couldn't stop the smirk that spread across my face. Her face flamed with anger or desire, I couldn't tell.

"You're going to pay for this when you let me go, I hope you know that. You won't sit for a week."

"You talk too much." I snapped and smacked my hand on her thigh. Her face went red and her jaw tightened. God, that power felt good. Was this how she felt every time she punished me? No wonder she liked it. I hopped off and stood next to the bed as I stripped her of her boxer briefs and tossed them aside, revealing her immaculately shaved pussy. Her legs were as muscular as her stomach. Years of playing soccer had left their mark.

I grabbed her left ankle and a restraint cuff, locking her leg into place. "By the time I'm done with you," I said in my surest, most dominant voice as I jerked her other leg hard, securing it to the bed, "you'll be the one who's asking for it."

I slid open the bottom drawer of Steph's side table. The 'fun drawer' as she called it. I shuffled through the contents and found a black, silky blindfold.

"Cas, I swear to God—" she protested.

I wrestled the eye mask over her head and adjusted it so I knew she could see nothing. I popped the side of her ass with my hand and she flinched away. "You'll call me Ma'am," I asserted.

She giggled, which infuriated me. I slid a long box from under the bed and took out Steph's favorite flogger. The strips of leather were so soft to the touch, but stung so fucking nicely when she slapped it across my bare skin.

"Give it up, Cassie," she chided. I slung the flog at her thighs where the strips landed with a pop, gently enough that I knew it didn't hurt her, but hard enough that her skin began to pink up.

"I said you'll call me Ma'am."

"Cassie, if you don't fucking turn me loose, I—"

I interrupted her with a slightly harder flog across her stomach and hips. I saw one tail tap her pussy and she gasped.

"Goddamn it, Cas," she said through gritted teeth.

I sighed. I slapped the flogger hard across her thighs and left it there while I unzipped my dress and let it fall to the floor. "Why do you have to be so difficult." I undid her ankles from the bed and in one swift motion flipped her onto her stomach, her hands still restrained above her head. I internally praised myself for my strength and relished in the power I felt seeing her pale, bare ass laid out for me on the bed. I reached back into the box under the bed and grabbed the spreader bar. I buckled the leather manacles to her ankles and tethered the middle of the bar to the cuffs holding her hands, putting her on her knees and elbows. I admired her ass and the view of her deliciously wet slit from behind as I climbed up to stand on the bed. She could pretend she didn't like what was happening all she wanted— her body told another story.

"Like I said," I began as I caressed her cheeks with my hand. "From this point forward, you'll call me Ma'am." I smacked the flogger hard across her ass, causing her to flinch. "And you'll do well to remember"—*smack*—"that when I give you a directive"—*smack*—"you'll do as I say the first time." *Smack*.

At the last blow Steph let out a whimper that sent heat through me. I adjusted my strap-on, pushing it against my clit and savoring the pressure.

"Do you understand?" I asked, pausing to let her answer.

She responded with silence.

"Stubborn girl," I moaned.

I laid into her, valuing this newfound authority. The first several licks she bit her lip and kept quiet, but eventually she was yelping at every lash. Her ass and lips were swollen and red, and her arousal was beginning to coat her inner thighs.

"Is that enough?" I asked, panting and drunk with

power.

"Yes," she whimpered. I gave her another hard stroke.

"Yes what?" I shouted.

"Yes, Ma'am!" she cried.

I smiled and stroked the silicone cock that, were it real, I knew would be bursting out of my panties. I stripped myself of the body-hugging spandex and let my member free. I lowered myself behind her and stroked the tip of it up and down her slick folds.

She let out a moan.

"You want me to fuck you, don't you?" I asked, taunting.

She pressed her ass up toward me and I backed away. "Yes, Ma'am," she groaned.

"Then what do you need to say?" I slapped the cock against her pussy and she yelped.

"Please," she panted, twisting her fingers into the sheets. With the very tip of the cock I pressed at her opening.

"Please, what?" She knew this game. She'd played it with me a million times before. God, it felt good to be on the other end.

"Please fuck me, Ma'am," she almost screamed.

I slammed into her and she cried out. Her ass was still warm from the spanking as I cupped it in my hands and thrust hard. Each time I plunged in, she moaned a little louder until her screams and my groans were a cacophony of ecstasy.

She bit down on the mattress to muffle her screams and I stopped suddenly, mid-thrust. Her ass crept back toward me, seeking the relief of orgasm.

I reached down and grabbed a handful of her short hair, pulling her head back. "Are you ready to come for me?" I barked.

"Yes… yes, Ma'am. Please, Ma'am."

That was exactly what I'd wanted. My tomboy, soft-butch, dominating, top of a girlfriend was malleable in my hands, ready to crumble at my next touch.

"I'm going to let you come. But I want to hear it," I growled. I entered her again and again, faster and harder than before, pulling back on her hair and letting my left hand reach around to find her clit.

She came hard, a stream of wetness coating my hand and the dildo. I released her hair and collapsed in a sweaty mess on top of her, gently trailing my fingers along her still-raised ass.

After what seemed like forever I rolled off of Steph, and unbuckled, unshackled, and unblindfolded her. We lay on our backs, staring at the spinning ceiling fan and trying to catch our breath. I suddenly felt very exposed with my pleasure-coated cock still rising up from my pelvis. I released the latches on the harness and began to remove it when Steph put her hand on mine, stopping me. I turned to look at her and she gently shook her head.

"Tomorrow, we'll go back to normal," she whispered. "Tonight's not over yet, Ma'am."

# THE ANTISOCIAL SISTER
## LUCY FELTHOUSE

Patricia unlocked the front door of her sister Maria's house and crept inside. She had no idea why she was creeping, though, considering no one was in. Which, of course, had been the whole point of her turning up the Saturday night before Christmas to deliver presents. Maria and her husband, Joe, would be at his work's Christmas do and their kids were at Joe's parents' house, leaving Patricia free and clear to do her Santa bit.

Only, as soon as she put the gift bags in her hands down and scurried along the hallway to turn the home security alarm off, she knew something was wrong. The alarm wasn't on. And not in a million years would either Maria or Joe leave the house empty without setting it. They were paranoid to the max, a situation exacerbated by all the warnings on TV and in the papers about scumbags breaking into homes at this time of year specifically to steal Christmas presents.

Therefore, Patricia came to the conclusion that either there was a burglary taking place at that very moment, and they'd managed to turn the alarm off, or there was, in fact, someone in. Neither situation was good, in her opinion, but as she tiptoed towards the living room, she wished heartily for the latter. Even a bollocking from her sister for sneaking into the house would be preferable to said sister being robbed.

Ready for either situation, she slipped her hand into her pocket to retrieve her phone, pulled it out and pressed the number nine three times—then kept her thumb hovering over the green button, just in case.

Carefully moving back and closing the front door—if

there was a burglary taking place, she didn't want to make it easy for the buggers to escape—Patricia then re-trod her steps, continuing towards the living room. A dim light shone from beneath the door—torchlight?

With her phone in a death grip, Patricia opened the living room door as quietly as possible, not wanting to alert any intruders to her presence, at least not until she'd phoned the police.

As the room beyond gradually came into view, Patricia mercifully neither heard nor saw any signs of anything untoward. Rather, she discovered that the source of light was coming from the television, as was a low-level murmuring. She frowned. Had Maria and Joe not gone to the Christmas party after all? But their car hadn't been parked out front...

"Hello?" she said, her tone tentative.

There was movement from the direction of the sofa, then a tousled dark head appeared over the back. "What the —oh... so you're the antisocial sister."

"Excuse me?" Patricia all but squeaked. "I'm the... what? And who the hell are you, and what are you doing here?"

"Hey," the dark-haired woman said quietly, "keep your voice down. The kids are asleep."

"The kids?" She turned and gently pushed the door shut behind her, then crossed the room and stood beside the sofa. Now she could see the woman in full—not that there was much of her. She was slim, petite—a boyish figure. Her cropped hair and clothes did nothing to dispel that idea, either. Patricia suspected this woman, whoever she was, frequently got mistaken for a member of the opposite sex. Not that it mattered—she was cute either way. She took a deep breath. "Could you please explain what's going on?"

Shifting from her reclined position into a sitting one, the woman patted the now-empty space beside her. "Of course. Sit down."

For reasons she couldn't quite fathom, Patricia did as she was told.

"I'm Renee," the tousle-haired cutie said. "I'm babysitting for the evening. I live a couple of doors down the road. As you probably know, the kids were meant to be with Joe's parents this evening, but Joe's dad came down with some kind of bug, I think. So I stepped in at the last minute."

"Oh."

"You sound disappointed."

"N—no. It's just that... when I saw the house alarm wasn't switched on..."

Renee quirked one shapely eyebrow. "You thought I was robbing the place, didn't you?"

Patricia's cheeks heated. "Maybe. Anyway, never mind that! What did you mean about me being the antisocial sister?"

A smirk playing on her lips, Renee replied, "Changing the subject much? But okay, I'll explain. Though I think it's pretty self-explanatory. Basically, when you're discussed in conversation, that's how you're described. Maria's the funny one, you're the antisocial one that never comes to parties, or turns up late, acts like a wallflower then leaves early. You get the idea. It's backed up by the fact I've known Maria and Joe for three years, since I moved here, and this is the first time we've met."

Patricia opened her mouth, then closed it again, realizing there was nothing she could really say to that. She couldn't even pretend that her feelings were hurt, because the facts didn't lie. She *did* avoid parties like the plague, and if somehow she ran out of excuses, or got guilt-tripped into attending, she would keep out of everyone's way as much as possible. It wasn't really being antisocial, though. It was more that she didn't like crowds. Give her a one-on-one conversation with someone and it was all good. A chat with a couple of good friends or family members; fine. But throw any more people into the mix and she was out of her comfort zone. She simply wasn't the sort of person who could hold court, talk loud and proud for anyone who cared to listen. Therefore melting into the background was her only option. And if she was going to do that, well then what was the point in attending?

Eventually, she gave what she hoped was a nonchalant shrug. "So I don't like parties. So what? We can't all like the same things, can we? Otherwise the world would be a very boring place."

"Hey," Renee said, holding her hands up. "No need to get all defensive on me. You asked the question, I answered it. Don't shoot the messenger."

"Humph," was all Patricia managed. Fixing her gaze on the television without actually seeing the flickering pictures, she wondered how she could extricate herself from this awkward situation. Somehow she sensed that simply announcing she was leaving wouldn't wash with Renee. There was a quiet intensity to the pixie-like woman, something that Patricia imagined would make her very difficult to defy, if not impossible.

She was just mentally berating herself for being so damn British—sitting there like a good, polite girl, instead of doing what she really wanted to do, which was go home— when Renee chipped in with, "You're kinda grumpy too, aren't you?"

"No," she shot back, "not at all. I just don't like having my personality and habits dissected by a total stranger, that's all." Standing abruptly, she continued, "Now if you'll excuse me, now I know you're not a burglar, I'll do what I came here to do, which was deliver Christmas presents, then I'll be on my way."

She resisted the temptation to stomp back out into the hallway, knowing she needed to keep quiet if she didn't want her niece and nephew to discover she was there. If they caught sight of Aunty Patricia then her chances of getting out of the house before Joe and Maria came home were nil. In fact, she'd probably be lucky to make it out before New Year's Eve. Instead she walked normally, opened the door to the hallway, picked up the gift bags, then retraced her steps to the living room.

Heading for the Christmas tree—gaudy and over-the-top as usual, as was her sister's preference—Patricia carefully placed the parcels down towards the back of the large pile. That way they wouldn't be spotted straight away, and the phone call to ask when she'd been round would be put off that little bit longer.

Straightening, she made for the door once more.

"What if we weren't total strangers?"

Renee's words stopped Patricia in her tracks, her hand in mid-reach for the door handle. She dropped it to her side. "Excuse me?"

Getting up, Renee crossed the room and quietly pushed the door shut. She remained standing very close to Patricia. "I said, what if we weren't total strangers?"

Patricia sighed. "Yes. I *heard* you, but once again I don't know what you *mean*."

"It's simple, really. You said you didn't like your personality and habits being dissected by a total stranger. So how about we get to know each other? Perhaps then you'll allow me to dissect you some more."

Patricia frowned and folded her arms across her chest. "And why on earth would you want to do that?"

"Because I know a little bit about you already, and I think you're *very* interesting."

"Oh, you do, do you? And what do you know, besides the fact I'm antisocial?"

"Well," Renee stepped closer still, and it took all of Patricia's willpower not to step back, not to show this cute pixie that she was intimidated by her, "I know, for example, that you're a lesbian. And that you're single…" She let her words tail off, and fixed Patricia with a gaze that was nothing short of wicked. And laden with intent.

Patricia gasped, not quite knowing whether it was Renee's words, or that *gaze* which had elicited her reaction. She repeated her earlier words. "So what?"

The other woman chuckled. "Oh, Patricia, do you really not get it?"

Her facial expression was obviously answer enough, because Renee paused only briefly before continuing, "I've been wanting to meet you for a while, you know. Ever since I knew you liked girls but didn't have a partner. I'd seen photos of you—I think you're hot, by the way—and the more I learned, the more intrigued I became. But you're a tough woman to pin down. So I bided my time. When your sister asked me to babysit tonight, I wondered if my patience would finally pay off. As far as *you* knew, the house would be empty, and as far as *I* knew, you hadn't brought the Christmas presents round yet. So, after all this time, a mixture of tenacity and coincidence has brought us together."

"Okay…" Patricia said. "So are you some kind of weirdo stalker, or what? Assuming you're getting at what I think you're getting at, surely there has to be an easier way to meet women."

Rolling her eyes, Renee then flashed her a good-natured grin. "Of *course* there is an easier way to meet women. There are lots of ways. But I didn't want to meet *women.* I wanted to meet *you.*"

The conversation had been weird since the moment it had begun, but now it was veering down the route of insane. Patricia idly wondered if perhaps she hadn't gone to her sister's at all, but had actually fallen asleep at home and was now enjoying a delightfully bonkers dream. But this was nuts even for her—she generally dreamt about people she knew. Not strangers.

Torn between her inadvisable attraction to the apparently crazy pixie and wanting to get away from said crazy pixie, Patricia remained rooted to the spot, the ache between her legs growing with every passing second. Fucking hell, talk about getting horny at inappropriate times. "And why's that?" she gritted out.

The good-natured grin turned hopeful. "Because I thought you and I would make a good match. At least once I can get past that defensive, suspicious shell of yours. I can see I'm going to have to be a bit heavy-handed, otherwise we'll both be old and grey by the time I've achieved that."

Patricia scowled. "Heavy-handed? Huh, I'd like to see you try."

Renee's eyes glinted. "Oh, really? Sounds like a challenge to me. Well, I accept." She paused, seemingly for dramatic effect. "Patricia… kneel down in front of me."

"Wha—" Patricia's mouth dropped open, but only part of the word came out, the rest stuck somewhere between her brain and her tongue.

The only response she got was a pair of pointedly raised eyebrows, the eyes beneath them steely and determined. Masterful.

In spite of herself, Patricia's knees began bending, and she felt a little bit like Alice, watching the world around her shoot up as she shrunk. Only she wasn't shrinking, just dropping to the mercifully thick carpet, then looking up at Renee, wide-eyed.

"Good girl."

Christ, the pixie's words and tone made it sound as though she was talking to a dog, not a person. Patricia should have been outraged, but in a bizarre twist of fate, her arousal grew. As did her need to please Renee. She didn't know where it had come from, or why, just that it existed.

"You up for some fun, Patricia?" Renee stood, hands on her hips, sassy as you like and waiting for a response.

Patricia narrowed her eyes—apparently her sudden obedience hadn't obliterated her common sense. "What kind of fun?"

"The kind of fun we'll both enjoy, that doesn't involve leaving this room, and won't wake the kids."

She couldn't really argue with that, could she? They were both adults… and who wouldn't want more fun in their lives? "Okay… but Maria and Joe—"

"Aren't due back for at least a couple more hours. And that's if it's a bad night. If it's a good night, they'll be out much later than that. So, do I take it that your answer is a yes?"

"Y—yes, it's a yes."

"Good girl," Renee said again, but this time her tone was more thoughtful than condescending, and Patricia found herself eagerly anticipating what was going to happen next. What precisely did the masterful pixie have in mind? And how the fuck could someone that looked like a pixie be masterful in the first place? Or should that be mistressful?

Patricia shook her head. Now she was making up words—probably not the best use of her time, when she should be pouring all of her concentration into the here and now. Luckily, Renee didn't seem to have noticed her lapse.

Rocking her weight—slight though it was—from one leg to the other, Renee said, "Okay, I have an idea. Strip your clothes from the top half of your body."

Still not quite knowing why, Patricia obeyed. Within moments her jacket, t-shirt and bra were in a pile next to her. It was only then she realized that, as well as her clit swelling and yearning for attention, her nipples were equally perky. They stood proud, pointing towards her tormentor, and she knew there was no way she'd be believed if she said they were behaving that way because it was cold.

"Nice," Renee commented, raking her gaze up and down Patricia's half-naked form, then licking her lips. Both actions ramped up Patricia's arousal further still.

"Okay," her tormentor said, stepping closer, "let's see what you're made of, shall we?"

With that, she leaned down a little, took Patricia's left

nipple between her thumb and fingers, and pinched hard.

Something between a gasp and a moan escaped Patricia's lips. Fuck, that had hurt!

Before she had chance for any further reaction, Renee repeated the action on Patricia's other nipple, a wicked grin on her face. "Normally I'm more into giving spankings and floggings, but given that wasn't an option this evening, I had to think outside of the box. And I'm very much enjoying it. Are you?"

Patricia's mind raced. She knew she'd been asked a question, but she was too busy trying to process the comment about spankings and floggings. Sensing that delaying her answer any longer would not end well for her, she blinked a couple of times, and eventually forced out, "Yes."

Was she, though? Was she enjoying being half-naked on her knees in her sister's living room, having her nipples pinched by a sadistic pixie?

The throbbing in triplicate from her clit and her nipples silently agreed with what she'd actually said.

"I like giving pain," Renee said, now using both hands to twist cruelly at Patricia's stiff nubs.

She stated what was now blatantly obvious, but Patricia kept the thought to herself. Renee hadn't asked a question, so there was no need to respond. She'd simply keep quiet and see how this bizarre situation played out.

"It gets me off," she continued, busily inflicting agony on Patricia's tits. She cupped them, squeezed them roughly, slapped them lightly—though Patricia suspected if she hadn't been trying to keep the noise down, she'd have been hitting much harder—scraped her nails over the sensitive flesh, and kept on with the pinching, pulling and rolling of the nipples.

By the time Renee stepped back in order to admire her handiwork, Patricia's chest felt like one giant throb. It burned and ached, a seemingly impossible mixture of pleasure and pain, and Patricia shifted uncomfortably, wishing she could do something to ease the yearning between her legs.

Apparently, it was not to be. Renee had other ideas. Smirking, she undid the belt on her skinny jeans, followed by the button and the zip. Shoving the material, along with her knickers, to her ankles, she kicked the garments off. She was now as naked on the bottom half as Patricia was on the top.

"On your back," Renee commanded.

Patricia complied. She had an inkling of what was going to happen next, and her mouth watered in anticipation. Her view was soon full of the sight of Renee, who firstly placed her feet either side of Patricia's head, then got to her knees.

The scent of pussy filled Patricia's nostrils, producing moisture from both her mouth and her own sex. She drew in a deep breath, delighting in the olfactory goodness, and waited. A moment later, she was rewarded as Renee settled directly over her face.

"Eat me, Patricia. Use your mouth—and your mouth only, mind—to make me come, and if you're good, I'll consider allowing you to come, too. But you have to be good, remember? Only good girls get presents at this time of year."

As far as Patricia was concerned, the opportunity to eat this gorgeous woman's pussy *was* her Christmas present. But if she could lick her way to earning a climax of her own, she certainly wasn't going to complain.

Shuffling into the optimum position, Patricia then reached up and cupped Renee's buttocks—which were warm, soft and firm all at the same time—and pulled her down onto her open and willing mouth. Immediately, she got to work. Her taste buds were quickly bathed in Renee's juices, and she let out a groan as she lapped and flicked, exploring her lover's vulva thoroughly in order to get a handle on what she liked, what she didn't, and, ultimately, what would make her climax.

It seemed Renee hadn't exaggerated when she said inflicting pain got her off, because Patricia had barely gotten into her stride when a series of muffled groans came from somewhere above her head, and Renee began rocking on her face, riding it almost. Patricia had gone from actively giving pleasure to simply having it taken from her, and she found she didn't mind, not one bit. All that mattered was the beautiful girl sitting on her face and the tangy juices coating her lips and seeping into her mouth. There was nothing more amazing to her than watching another woman climax, and although she'd been given little choice in the matter, she was happy to lie back and enjoy the show.

All too soon, the show was at an end. Renee shuffled off of Patricia's face and settled onto the carpet in a heap, breathing heavily.

Unsure what to do next, Patricia sat up, drawing her knees to her chest in an attempt to cover up. She didn't want to make the next move and get it wrong, but nor did she want their encounter to end there. She wanted more, so much more. The whole thing could have been written up and placed as the definition of 'out of the blue' in a dictionary, but although she had no answers yet—it would take a while of sifting through her own thoughts and feelings on this—she knew one thing for sure: it had been the hottest experience of her life to date. Further exploration was definitely on the agenda, whether it was with Renee or not, but first she had to deal with her immediate future.

Just then, a rattle and a burst of laughter came from the direction of the front door. Fuck—Maria and Joe were home! Patricia and Renee looked at each other, horrified, then leapt into action. Knowing that putting a bra on at speed was impossible, Patricia ignored it and reached for her t-shirt, pulling it on, followed by her jacket. Then she retrieved her bra and stuffed it into her jacket pocket, pulling the zip to keep it secure.

A glance over at Renee revealed she wasn't having quite such success at speedy dressing. In her post-orgasmic haze, she'd barely gotten her feet back into her jeans.

Patricia made a snap decision. Stepping to Renee, she planted a quick kiss on her lips, murmured, "Get my number from Maria," then moved for the living room door. Opening it just enough to slip through, she said loudly—though not so loud the kids would hear—"Sorry to have disturbed your film, Renee. If you could let Maria and Joe know—oh!"

Her forward motion carried her into the hallway, where she pulled the door closed behind her. "Hi, guys," she said, glad that Maria and Joe were more than a little drunk, and therefore hadn't yet gotten as far as turning on the hall light. "You're back early. Did you have a good night? I was just in the area, so I thought I'd pop in and drop your presents off. They're under the tree. How's your dad doing, Joe? Renee said he's not well…"

She was waffling, of course, but was hopefully buying Renee enough time to get herself sorted out.

As her sister and brother-in-law blinked at her confusedly, she realized they were more inebriated than she'd first thought. "Right!" she said brightly, retrieving her keys from where she'd left them on the hall table, "I'll get going, then. Talk to you soon. Bye, guys!"

Escaping into the cold night, her breath misting in front of her, Patricia stifled a giggle. It was probably more hysteria than amusement, but she didn't care. She just hoped Renee had managed to make herself decent before the drunkards had gone into the living room.

She glanced back at the house as she slid into the driver's seat of her car. The front door opened, and Renee slipped out, grinning, and headed straight for Patricia's car.

Huh, it looked like the evening wasn't over yet. But was she going to get her present? She pressed the button to open the car window, guessing she'd find out soon enough.

And well, if she hadn't yet earned it, she was more than

willing to make up the difference.

# ONE HUNDRED STROKES
## SINCLAIR SEXSMITH

"May I sit?" Morgan's voice surprises Elise; she hadn't seen her approach. She looks up from her book and blinks, then composes her face and her answer at once.

"Are your chores complete?"

"Yes, Ma'am."

"Tell me." This is their ritual every night, the way they love to come back together. Elise's eyes sparkle as she fights the urge to reach out and grab her, pull her into her lap. Rituals are important, she reminds herself. Not only to display her authority, though yes that too, but also to remind her of all that she does, the many ways she is devoted. Elise stays more present in gratitude and strives more successfully to be worthy when she pays attention to their rituals.

Morgan begins the list. "Your tea service is complete; the dishes are done and put away; your clothes and jewels are put away, and tomorrow's are laid out for you. Sir Elvis Purrmeister has been fed."

Elise feels a smile pull on the corners of her mouth, starts to suppress it, and lets it come. Her cat's name is just Elvis, but Morgan has taken to adding the honorific and surname, and Elise is too amused to have her change it. It is clear who is above whom in the hierarchy, anyway, so the proper respect is just one more thing to admire about Morgan.

"Tomorrow's schedules, both yours and mine, are next to the bed and the morning alarms are set. The bed is turned down. And, I have picked tonight's implement. It is in the usual place on the nightstand." Morgan doesn't look smug or tired, just pleased to be useful and grateful to be serving.

Elise sighs a little, with relief and relaxation, with the pleasure of being taken care of precisely as she likes it. "Good job, boy; you may sit." She pats the side of her thick leather reading chair and Morgan takes her seat at her Mistress's feet, leaning against her bare legs and cuddling into her with happy sighs, the tension from the day visibly leaving her shoulders.

Elise takes another sip of her tea and goes back to her book—one of those classic English novels that she likes. This one is *Pride and Prejudice*, a favorite she re-reads once a year or so. This is the second time Morgan has seen it in her hands.

Most nights, this is how it goes. Sometimes Morgan has a book, or something to study, or some lines to write for training or task. Usually, Elise has a novel, something that feels indulgent but keeps her mind steady and her heart thrumming. She likes to be as far into the adult-land in the evenings as possible—spending all day with preschoolers and kindergarteners for her job is exhausting, and can take such a toll.

She fingers the hair on the back of Morgan's head absently, as if fingering a blanket on the chair or her own sweater. Her submissive's presence is comforting, reassuring. The warm mint tea and honey soothes her and flows golden down her tongue. Everything is just right.

After a few more chapters, when Lydia elopes with Mr. Wickham, Elise closes the book with a small snap and stands. Morgan blinks and quickly rises to her ready position —hands behind her back, eyes down. She does not stay seated when Elise is standing. Elise pulls Morgan close, nuzzles cheek against forehead, and Morgan wraps her arms around Elise's waist. How well they fit together, their bodies' contours so complimentary. She holds her there for a moment until she says, "Okay; bedtime, boy," and they separate. She turns to the hall to go into the bathroom for some of her evening self-care, and Morgan goes to the bedroom to strip. Elise takes her time—brushing and braiding her hair, applying cleansers and creams to her skin, brushing her teeth. Morgan waits. The waiting is like meditation, but cleaner for her, as it is totally beyond her control and thus much easier for her to let go. This is the kind of thing she tells her Mistress in her journal, which Elise reads weekly.

Morgan has picked out the thick wooden paddle, taller than Elise's hand's widest spread. One side is soft suede; the other is hard wood. The handle is wrapped so her hand is protected.

This paddle makes beautiful, deep bruises.

When she enters, Morgan has taken off her t-shirt and boy shorts, the ones that almost show the bottoms of the cheeks of her ass. She's down to a jock strap, the white one, on her knees, hands behind her back in her submissive meditation position next to the bed. She knows to wait there until Elise releases her. Elise can see Morgan breathing in deeply, chest in heaves, jaw working as she swallows down the saliva that is pooling in her mouth. So many nights of this ritual, so many repeated patterns with their evening beatings that Morgan starts to flinch involuntarily when Elise gets close. She is a trained pet. Elise can see her arousal in the flushing of her nearly naked skin, the slight hardening of her nipples. Elise is nearly naked now, too, down to one thin cream-colored slip with nothing beneath it. Her feet are bare. She keeps her bedroom warm.

"Here." She points to the bed. She is not cruel, not really—just direct, specific. She eliminates superfluousness. She does not believe in coddling in D/s; she believes in trust, agency, consent. She believes Morgan's deep desire to serve and to please, and she is grateful, yes, but she also feeds off of it. She consumes it like cotton candy, leaving her mouth pink around the edges and her fingers sticky. She needs it, just as Morgan does. Her clipped tone is only for simplicity, and for intimacy, as she trusts Morgan not to need handholding. Not anymore.

Mistress Elise Winter is deft with a paddle. It was always one of her favorites when she was Domming professionally, delivering such a satisfying smack and leaving such good bruises. Plus, it can be a key prop in any age-play scene: just a few words and it is suddenly a cutting board the bottom's mom grabbed from the kitchen, or a fraternity paddle stolen by a sorority girl, or a headmistress's prized discipline tool. Even more than obedience, Elise likes her subs small and little, with feigned innocence. Something about the corruption just works with the way she is wired.

She whispers in Morgan's ear before she begins— something soothing, something that makes her relax, arch her ass in the air a little higher, and lean in to Elise just a fraction of an inch more. Elise rubs herself against her ass and thighs, her hand stroking the fine muscles of her back. When she whimpers a little, Elise knows she is ready.

Starting with her hands, she warms up Morgan's ass and thighs and upper back. She is chest-down, face kissed by the burgundy 1000-count sheets, her feet just touching the floor of Elise's raised bed. When Elise moves from the quick light swats to the deeper fist-thuds, Morgan asks her if it is time.

"Yes, go ahead and start," she replies.

Morgan begins counting aloud. Elise will do twenty or thirty more with her hands before bringing in the paddle to finish the hundred strokes.

They don't say much. It's just one of those quiet nights. Elise tries to let her job fall away, the stresses of her vanilla life out of sync with her kinky self, the projects for the non-profit board she sits on, the pressure of her mother's struggling health battle with emphysema. Nothing precisely fills Elise's mind, but she finds her inner world quite full when she quiets and focuses. The relief of a target, a victim, is almost enough to make her start crying; the release feels so huge, like a dam beginning to leak and ready to smash apart with the weight of what is held back.

Morgan is counting. "Thirty-two... thirty-three... thirty-four." She is diligent, and taking it all for Elise. She is deconstructing and reassembling in front of Elise's eyes in that way that power and sensation can inspire. Elise slides the paddle into her grip and opens a rain of blows on Morgan's tender flesh, already pink and warm to the touch. Morgan's breathing gets heavier and her voice more strained. Elise doesn't care; they have only just reached fifty. She winds up like a baseball batter and swings.

Morgan screams into the sheets. Drops of sweat form and trickle at her neck, at the small of her back. Her ass is a round handful and Elise takes her grip as it pleases her, kneading like dough. She leans down to bite Morgan's ass. Morgan yells out, "Mistress, please, oh god, please, it hurts!" She squirms away, but Elise's hands hold her hips. She leaves a dark ring mark from her teeth; that one will bruise up nicely.

She licks her lips, and swats with the paddle again.

"This is for me, not you," she whispers, mostly to herself. "I need it, I don't know why I need it, but I need it, need your ass like this, need my marks on you, need your ache to show in your face tomorrow when you sit down."

"Sixty-eight... sixty-nine... seventy." She is panting between the numbers. Elise is taking her time, savoring each one. Morgan's ass is already purple—she won't be able to sit. Elise focuses on her thighs. Morgan is trying so hard not to squirm. Elise slips a finger between her ass cheeks to check on her hole: it flexes against her finger pad like a kiss, open and eager.

"Hungry boy," she murmurs, swatting again with her right hand. Morgan whimpers, pushing back against her just a little, not wanting to be too eager or demanding, but showing she wants it.

Her knees are getting weak. The bed holds her up. Elise strokes Morgan's hair and she turns so one cheek is on the bed and she can see her Mistress, just a little. Elise's thick braid is flying behind her like the tail of a kite, her hands moving quickly, opening Morgan's tight back hole as the paddle slams in to her. She tries with all her concentration to keep count. She misses a few, but Elise lets it go; she is doing so well. "So good, boy," she coos. "You're so good."

She's in the nineties now and they are both climbing. Elise's two fingers dip into the Boy Butter on the nightstand and open her hole just enough for the pressure to distract Morgan from the wicked paddle. She might let Morgan get off. Will she? She can't decide. She likes it when she comes.

"Ninety-eight... ninety-nine... one hundred," Morgan is whimpering each number, tears down her beautiful cheeks, body shuddering in waves of release. Elise steps back and breathes, separates herself from Morgan for a moment so they can both catch their breath. Her wrists throb, her shoulders buzz with aliveness. A few hairs have strayed and she tucks them back into her braid.

"Morgan," she says softly. "Get on the bed and turn over."

She does, slowly, testing out how her muscles have been changed, wincing at the rawness. Elise slides her slip up her thighs and kneels on the bed, swinging her leg over Morgan and sliding up her submissive's body.

"Oh god," Morgan says, muffled, before Elise has even lowered her cunt onto her mouth to feed it to her. Elise's cunt is a hungry mouth, too, swollen and wet, dripping. She never lets Morgan enter her, but she uses her mouth when she wants. Morgan's stamina is impressive.

She lifts her slip just enough so it is out of the way, not restricting the openness of her thighs. Its hem kisses Morgan's forehead. She laps with her tongue, sucks with her lips and throat. Elise's clit is huge and bursting with need, angry and red like the palms of her hands, like Morgan's ass. Elise needs it, this release, maybe even more than Morgan does—though how can they compare? But her want is monstrous, never-ending. She almost feels like herself again. She rocks her hips over her sub's mouth and steadies herself on the headboard, arms outstretched. She barely remembers there is a person under her right now, she just grinds down and against this beautiful boy, this toy who always does it just right, just right there.

"Come when I do," she orders, low and fast, not giving much warning—but Morgan won't need it. She's been ready to come since her ass was fingered. And she knows what Elise sounds like, what it means when she starts clawing at her hair and suffocating her with her hole.

"Fuck, that's it, there, god oh god oh *god*!" Elise is sitting on a volcano and erupts through her mouth with words and grunts and screams when she comes, heavy, filling Morgan's mouth with liquid, pushing it into her throat. She opens wide and takes it, shuddering under her and swallowing.

"Thank you, Mistress, thank you," Morgan repeats, breathless, still only breathing small sips of air.

Elise moves off of Morgan and collapses onto the pillows; she curls up in her arms.

"Stay in my bed tonight," she says, stroking Morgan's hair.

"Yes, Ma'am," Morgan sighs, pulling the covers up over them both as they drift off to sleep.

# THE ENCOUNTER
## EDEN DARRY

I saw her walk in and take a seat at the bar. Blonde hair, high breasts and long legs. Gorgeous. Others had noticed her as well, and I watched as they sized her up and considered making a play. I hung back. I wanted to see them approach her, watch as they sauntered up, cocksure and arrogant. I knew she would turn them away. I laughed out loud as she didn't even bother to glance at the first one—a tall woman with dark close-cropped hair and tats all up her arms. She sent her on her way with a flick of her hand and a shake of her head—like she was waving away a troublesome fly.

The next one would probably be a little more to her taste, I guessed. Still tall, but not quite so arrogant, dressed all in leather and panther-sleek. Still the woman at the bar shook her head, and turned to catch the bartender's attention instead. The other woman was left talking to her back, and I watched as she looked around to see if anyone had witnessed her humiliation, before she slunk off to re-join her friends.

I waited a little longer, telling myself that I wanted to look at her a little more—she was beautiful—when the truth was, I was afraid that I might be turned away too. Although I knew exactly what she wanted—what she needed—doubt lingered and I was surprised to realize that I needed another drink to line my spine, before I would be confident enough to approach her. This was the woman I had been waiting for all night. The woman I dreamed about. My perfect fantasy come to life before my eyes, and I really didn't want to fuck it up.

I downed my scotch, barely noticing as it burned a fiery path down my throat. I wiped my sweaty palms on my jeans, and, checking the coast was clear, I made my way over to her. It would have been more than awkward to arrive at her bar stool at the same time as another hopeful contender. I took a deep breath, got my head in the game, and made my move.

"Are you looking to play?" I leaned in close to her, my lips brushing the shell of her ear. I felt her stiffen, and to my relief, relax again.

"Maybe I am."

I stood still, permitting her inspection of me as she looked me up and down, her gaze leaving hot trails over my body. She flicked her eyes over me one last time, resting briefly on my crotch, and then up again.

She took a sip, placed the drink on the bar and signaled for another. "What did you have in mind?"

I looked around the room, meeting the eyes of one of the women she had rebuffed. The other woman stared at me openly, challengingly. I stared back, eyes hard and ready for it —after all, these were the rules of our particular game. Survival of the fittest, and you guarded what was yours—or what you wanted to be yours—and I knew that blonde would dismiss me without thought if she decided that I was anything less than she needed me to be.

The would-be suitor looked away at last, and I was relieved because my eyes were beginning to burn with the effort of not blinking.

I turned my attention back to the blonde who was smiling a small, secret smile, and I knew she had witnessed the contest. I hoped she was satisfied with the display.

"I have a hotel room close to here. Let's go." I said it confidently, even though inside I was terrified she might say no, that she'd rebuff me and move on to someone more obviously butch. To emphasize my point, I gripped the back of her neck and leaned close, "Tonight, you belong to me." I felt her shiver, felt her body bow a little under my hand, and that was when I knew for sure that she had chosen me.

The night air was frigid, and I pulled her closer to me as we stepped outside. She slipped her arm under my coat and around my waist and leaned in to steal my warmth. It felt good to have her there, to be able to provide her with something that she needed. I put my arm around her shoulders, and despite the fact that she was slight, I sensed the strength in her body. I loved that about her. She was at once delicate, with a long graceful neck and finely shaped cheekbones, and also strong, with powerful legs that were at the moment, encased in black stockings. Her rounded ass spoke of time spent working out. I touched it now, allowing my hand to move over it in a brief caress. I imagined it without the skirt that covered it, imagined skimming my hands over the firm, soft flesh and delving into the cleft, to the tight muscle that was hidden there.

My clit jerked in my jeans, and she must have felt me shudder, because I heard her laugh, and when I glanced down, her face was turned up to mine, that knowing smile playing gently on her full lips. I could hardly wait to get her into my hotel room, but before that, I needed to get it together. She was with me because she needed my control. Craved my iron will that would bend her and twist her. And she had to be confident that I wouldn't break her. I could never show her my uncertainty, or how close she had me to losing control, or she would never trust me to dominate her.

We were near the hotel now and I needed to lay down the rules. I had to walk in there in complete control. I pulled her into an alley, pushed her roughly against the wall and grasped her jaw in my hand. I leaned close, close enough to kiss, and I wanted to kiss her. I was dying to push my bigger body hard against hers and claim her mouth, bruise her lips with mine. But, I didn't. Instead, I put my mouth to her ear, much like I had earlier in the bar, and I felt her pelvis push into mine for a moment.

"Once we get inside, there'll be no more talking unless I ask you a question. Once we get inside, you're mine. You'll do exactly what I tell you to and nothing else. Understand?"

"Yes." She didn't hesitate.

"I'm going to fuck you," I jerked my crotch into her, fast and hard, "in your mouth and in your pussy and in your ass." She gasped as my hand reached up and pinched her nipple under her coat. "If you don't do exactly as I say, I'm going to punish you and I won't go easy on you. If I do anything you don't like, the password is Cody."

She looked at me then, eyebrow raised, and repeated, "Cody?"

"Yeah. Problem?"

"No, no problem." Remembering her role, she lowered her eyes. *Good.*

"Let's go." I had to stop myself from dragging her into the hotel and running with her into my room. I wanted her badly, and I couldn't show her that, and it was killing me.

The elevator took forever to come and when it finally did, it seemed to take an age to get to my floor. I was careful not to jam the key card into the slot. I didn't want her to see how out of control I was. I almost cried with relief when the green light showed up and I ushered her into the room ahead of me.

I'd splurged a little and booked a suite instead of just a room. The door opened onto a good-sized sitting room, with double doors leading through to a bedroom with a king-sized bed. I hoped that she didn't mind—that she liked it. I was afraid to look at her in case she didn't approve, and I was in control here, so I avoided her gaze. In line with the rules, she didn't speak. She waited obediently for me to instruct her further. It made me hot—hotter than I was already—to be in complete control of her. Knowing that this beautiful, smart woman trusted me to lead her was the biggest turn-on in the world.

"Stand over there, by the couch," I instructed, my clit already swelling in anticipation. "That's good. I want you to kneel on it, face the back." She did as told without a word. I was behind her now. I pushed the coffee table out of the way. "Hike up your skirt above your knees. Are you wearing panties?"

She hesitated for a moment. Then, nodded her head.

"Show me."

She pulled her skirt up high on her thighs, exposing only the tops of her creamy, long legs. She had on black stockings—the kind that held themselves up—and I could just about tell that she was wearing a G-string. I swallowed hard; my mouth and throat had gone completely dry. She was amazing. "Higher. Pull it up higher. You're a bad girl, aren't you? Did you wear that on purpose? Did you know you were going to get fucked tonight? Answer me."

"I… I hoped that I would." She still didn't turn around, and her voice was small. I was surprised because she had been so confident in the bar, and now she seemed unsure. "Hey. Look at me." I said it softly—not strictly within the rules, but I wanted to see her face. She turned around then, her eyes to the floor. She looked nervous as hell. "It's okay. You're beautiful. Do you know that? How beautiful you are?"

She smiled then. Just a small one, but enough to let me know she was okay. "Turn around now. I want to see your ass. I want to see that tight, round ass. I want to see what I'm going to be fucking soon." I hardened my voice. Even though I was about ready to come in my jeans, I sounded cool and confident, and she needed that.

She bent forward, leaning against the cushions on the back of the couch. The skirt rode up a little higher and I saw the bottoms of her ass cheeks. "Are you wet? Answer me."

"I… yes."

"Show me."

She turned around again, unsure of what I wanted her to do. She didn't speak though, and that was good. She remembered not to talk without permission. She was a quick learner, but it might prove to be a problem later. I wanted to punish her—she would want to be punished. I'd have to make up a reason to do it, or she'd need to break the rules. Either way, it didn't matter. Later on, she was going to get her ass paddled.

"Put your finger inside yourself. I want to see how wet you are. Put it inside your pussy and then come here."

She did as I asked, coming to stand in front of me, her index finger glistening with the evidence of her arousal. "Suck it. Lick it all off." I watched as she ran her tongue slowly up her finger and made a moaning sound deep in her chest. I was close enough to see her pupils dilate and her nostrils flare. I knew this look—this look said that she was turned on, and that she wanted to come. Soon.

Before she'd finished, I grabbed her hand, forced it down between her legs where her skirt had stayed hitched. Careful not to be too rough, I pushed her finger into the folds of her sex and then brought it back up for my inspection. I brought it close to my nose and then sampled the juices that coated it, with the very tip of my tongue. She was sweet and salty, and I loved the taste of her.

"Okay, back on the couch like before. Slide those panties off—if you can even call them panties. Good. Now, lean forward over the back of it. Yeah, like that. Spread your legs. I want to see your pussy. That's good, you're doing real good. God, you're wet. And swollen. Do you want me to fuck you?"

"Yes."

"Beg me then. I want you to beg me to fuck you. Can you do that?"

I knew she wouldn't. Knew it as soon as I saw her back stiffen. She wasn't ready to beg yet, and that was good. "I gave you an order. I told you that I wanted you to beg me to fuck you. Can you do that? Do it. Now." Still nothing. I smiled. This would be driving her crazy. I could almost hear the words 'go fuck yourself' on the tip of her tongue. I wanted to laugh, but I didn't—I couldn't. If I laughed, I knew she really would tell me to go and fuck myself, and then the game would be over.

"Okay. This isn't good news for you. You disobeyed me, and I won't be disobeyed. Not by you. That's my pussy you've got over there, and when I tell you to do something, you'll fucking do it. Get up."

She got up. Stood before me with her eyes to the floor. I could almost feel the excitement coming off of her. She knew what was coming next, and she wanted it bad. "Go to that bag over there. See it? In the bedroom? Bring it here."

When she placed the bag at my feet, where I'd moved to sit on the couch, I instructed her to open it. I wanted her to see the array of toys in there. Handcuffs and strap-ons and butt plugs. I'd gone a little crazy in the sex store and picked a bunch of stuff out. I doubted that I'd get to use it all tonight, but that didn't matter. There would be other nights.

"Take out the paddle. Good, now hitch your skirt all the way up." She was standing directly in front of me, I could smell how turned on she was. "Open yourself. Show me that clit. Nice. Now, rub it for me. Oh, yeah, that's good." I leaned back into the couch and watched as she drew her finger in small circles around her clit, the other hand still holding the paddle. I wanted to grab her hips and pull her to my mouth, but I didn't. I watched as her breathing deepened and she moaned softly. Her finger was soon joined by another, both moving faster and faster as she began to climax.

"Stop."

"What?" Her eyes flew open, but her fingers continued circling her clit.

"I said stop." I pushed her hand away and then, slapped her pussy. Not too hard, but not softly either. Her eyes widened, and then narrowed. I sensed her about to say something—probably about to call me an asshole—but she didn't in the end. Remembering the game we were playing, she dropped her eyes to the floor. I couldn't help myself, I reached out and ran my finger between her folds, grasped her clit gently and ran it between my fingers. Her pelvis jerked and she pushed into my hand.

"That's enough. Now, come here and lie over my lap. You disobeyed me and I have to punish you. Good. Okay, scoot up a little. That's good. Remember, 'Cody', if you want me to stop." She didn't answer, so I guessed we were good to go. I looked at her ass, lying there over my lap. I ran my hand over the soft swell of it, and down along the cleft. I pushed gently into the space between and found the tight ring of muscle. It was already wet from her juices, so it didn't need any lubrication. I followed the outline of it gently and felt her squirm in my lap. "You like that?"

"Yes."

"Well, then I'd better stop. I'm supposed to be punishing you." I almost laughed at the sound of her 'hmph' beneath me.

Without warning, I brought the paddle down on her ass. It wasn't hard, but I guess the shock of it was enough to make her cry out. I used my hand to smooth over her cheeks which were already turning red. I brought it down a second time, a little harder, but still only enough to make it sting. I paddled her three more times in quick succession before I judged it was enough. Her ass was bright red and must have been stinging pretty badly, but she hadn't made a sound since that first time. I was proud of her.

"Get up." She stood quickly, bare from the waist down, her pussy swollen and wet. "I've got a feeling you enjoyed that. Did you? Did you like it when I spanked your ass? Answer me."

"No."

"I don't believe you. Get on your knees." For a second, I thought she wouldn't. Not because she didn't want to, but because she didn't like being told what to do. I was relieved when she dropped to her knees in front of me. "Unzip me.

Pull my jeans down." I lifted my hips so she could get them down around my knees, and slid a little closer to the edge of the couch. "Now, you're going to eat my pussy. You'd better do a good job too. With that mouth, you've got no excuse not to. Get to it."

\* \* \*

She smelled good enough to eat. And I was happy to be eating her. I hadn't been sure about tonight at all. I had played with the idea of being submissive before, a little spanking here, a little bondage there. But this was new. Putting myself in someone else's control wasn't something I was used to.

When I'd seen her walk up to me at the bar, my reservations had disappeared. She was perfect—my Domme fantasy come to life—and I had found myself getting wet just at the sight of her standing in front of me, so confident and sure.

The hotel suite was something else though. It must have cost a fortune and seemed like a waste for one night. But, as I'd knelt on the couch, showing her my pussy and listening to her suck in a breath behind me that she thought I hadn't heard, I decided that it was perfect. The whole night was exactly right, and I wanted to return the gift she was giving to me. I wanted to be the submissive that she had dreamed of.

I could hear her breathing becoming more labored above me, as I licked her slowly. I took my time, circling gently around her clit. A quick flick up one side of her inner fold, and then the other. She groaned above me, her hips beginning a familiar steady rhythm, as she took my head between her hands and pulled me harder into her.

"Oh God, baby, that feels so good. You're so good at licking pussy. Yeah, just like that." I smiled into her crotch and began to quicken my pace. She groaned again, grinding more insistently and I could feel that she was close to coming. Glancing up quickly, I could see that her eyes were squeezed shut, so I moved my hand down to my own aching clit. It was wet and swollen, and I needed to come so badly. I didn't think she'd notice, but the next thing I knew, she had pulled herself out of my mouth and was watching me with a half smile on her lips.

Part of me was pleased—it might mean another spanking—but I was so heavy and wet, and I didn't think that I had ever needed to come so much before.

"Did you think I wouldn't notice?" Her voice was soft and her eyes shone. I could tell that she was happy I'd disobeyed her. "Answer me." She grasped my chin gently, shaking it slightly.

"I… I'm sorry."

"That's not what I asked. I asked if you thought I wouldn't notice you servicing your own pussy—*my* pussy, really."

"I didn't think you'd mind." My clit was tingling in anticipation of what might come next.

"Well, I guess we're going to have to address that, aren't we?"

I didn't answer her as she hadn't given me permission to speak—God, even that turned me on. And, I was surprised. In my real life, I didn't ask anybody's permission for anything. At work especially, they usually asked me.

She sighed. "Go to the bag. I want you to take out the cock and harness and bring them to me. Now."

Jesus, I was excited. I'd used a dildo before, but the one I had seen in the bag earlier was bigger than anything I'd ever had inside me. My pussy ached for it, to feel her inside me, pounding me until I couldn't think.

I brought her the equipment, and stood in front of her, waiting. My skirt was still hitched up around my waist, exposing my lower half completely. I felt my juices coating my inner thighs and I knew she could see it too.

She seemed to consider for a moment, before standing.

"Take your clothes off. All of them. Now." I did as she asked. Slowly, I pulled my shirt over my head, baring my lacy black bra which showed just a shadow of the nipples beneath. "Nice." I heard her whisper. Then, I dragged down my skirt, leaving me in nothing except my stockings and heels. Her eyes were bugging out of her head, and I was pleased. I'd gone to a lot of trouble this evening in the hopes of getting that very reaction.

"Go over to the couch, around the back. Brace yourself on it and wait for me." I did as she asked, leaning forward so my head was pillowed in my arms and my ass in the air. "Now, spread your legs. Yeah, just like that." Then, she was behind me, running her hands over my ass, between my legs to cup me firmly. Then her fingers were inside me—finally. I could feel the rough rub of her denim as she finger fucked me—stretching me out and opening me up. Not that I needed much working on—I had been ready for a long time.

She bent close to my ear and I could smell peppermint and a hint of the scent she wore.

"I'm going to fuck you now. That's what you want, isn't it? This big cock sliding in and out of your swollen pussy?" I didn't answer, but my breath hitched in excitement. "Oh yeah, you want it. You just soaked my hand. I am going to fuck you until you can't see. Until you can't think. Until the only thing you know is me. Pounding your pussy with my cock and fucking your ass with my fingers."

I almost came right then in anticipation. Suddenly, her strong hand gripped my neck while the other guided the cock into me. I felt myself stretch to accommodate it, and then it filled me just like she'd promised it would. I cried out from the pleasure, and felt her stiffen and start to withdraw, concerned that she was hurting me. "No! Stay! Oh God, fuck me. Fuck baby. Please." I barely recognized myself, but I couldn't bear the thought of her pulling out and leaving me empty.

The next thing I knew, she was fucking me blind. She slammed the cock in and out of me in a steady rhythm. One hand still held me down—not that I needed to be—while the other rubbed gently against my asshole. She dipped her finger in my juices and used it to lubricate my passage, a gentle finger probed for entrance.

Soon, I could feel her pushing into both holes simultaneously, and I didn't think I'd ever been filled quite so thoroughly. I heard someone groaning and grunting and begging for more, and was surprised to realize that it was me. Soon, I was coming. Harder than I'd ever come in my life. The ecstasy washed over me, as everything tightened, went rigid, and then collapsed into a boneless jelly.

I couldn't see or think or hear. All I knew was her, catching me as I fell. Pulling me close and gently bringing me down, cradling me on the floor, against the back of the couch. Then, all I could feel was her, as she stroked my hair and kissed my temple. And all I could hear was her, as she whispered to me that she loved me, that I was beautiful and wonderful.

"That was amazing." These were the first words out of my mouth as we lay snuggled in the huge hotel bed. It was my favorite position, on my side and nestled into her shoulder so I could stroke the soft skin on her chest.

"Ummm." I could tell that she was wasted too.

"Baby, can we stay here forever?" I knew we couldn't, but I had to ask.

"Sure, why not? The kids can live with your mom, and Kay can have the dogs." She smiled down at me, to let me know that she wasn't serious.

"Did you remember that Dee has gymnastics practice tomorrow?"

"Yeah. Your mom has the kids until the afternoon—and I got us a late check out." She snuggled closer, and sighed. That meant she was getting ready to go to sleep, I knew.

"Baby?"

"Ummm?"

"Did you enjoy tonight?" I felt silly asking. I knew that she had, but the whole experience had left me feeling raw—exposed somehow. I felt her draw me closer and kiss the top of my head.

"You are beautiful and amazing, and I am so pleased that we did this. What about you? Are you okay with it? I didn't hurt you or anything?" I heard the concern in her voice and smoothed my hand over her chest to reassure.

"It was the best sex of my life. I want to do it again. Soon."

"We will. I promise." She sighed again and I slapped her chest. "Hey! What was that for?"

"*Cody*? You made our safe word, the *dog's* name?"

She laughed. "I completely forgot to think of one. It was the first thing that came into my head."

"I'm just glad it wasn't one of the kids' names."

"Oh, that's gross!" She pulled me tighter—the way she did when she wanted to go to sleep. I think she thought if she cut off my air supply, I wouldn't be able to talk anymore.

"Baby?"

"Yeah?"

"I love you."

"I love you too. Go to sleep now."

I snuggled tighter into her, loving the way she felt. Soft and warm and strong. And all mine. Tonight had been the best sex of my life, and I couldn't wait to do it all again. After twelve years and two kids, I loved her more than I ever had. I felt closer in some way by sharing this with her—by giving over all of my control to her. I had trusted her to take care of me, and she hadn't disappointed. I fell asleep feeling sore and wasted and completely loved.

# SECRETLY SUBMISSIVE
## BROOKE WINTERS

The submissive squirmed below me as Vanessa sent another jolt of electricity through the violet wand, to the submissive's pussy. As her tongue flicked out over my clit I imagined that I was in her place. I imagined that I was the one tied down, that it was my pussy at Vanessa's mercy. I closed my eyes to block out the reality, pretended that it was Vanessa's mouth pleasuring me, that I was her focus. My orgasm built as images of Vanessa flew through my mind. Vanessa spanking me. Vanessa demanding that I pleasure her. Vanessa tying me up. I imagined being bound and helpless.

As I came down from my orgasm Vanessa caught my eye and smiled, her own gaze clouded with arousal. I moved away from the submissive, suddenly feeling empty. Right back to where I was before we had started the scene. Desperate, wanting, scared.

I made my way towards the bar, content that Vanessa would take care of the submissive and I wouldn't be missed.

Four shots later, I knew there wasn't enough alcohol to fill the void. I kept drinking anyway. Who the hell was going to stop me? Certainly not Vanessa. She was busy with that woman. Vanessa was probably snuggled up somewhere with… what was her name? I could barely remember my own name, I certainly couldn't remember Vanessa's latest sub.

Vanessa would barely notice that I was gone. She wasn't going to turn that stern gaze on me and tell me that I'd had enough. She wasn't going to spank me for getting drunk. Vanessa just didn't care.

The night passed in a blur of shots and dancing. I remember Chloe offering me a lift home. I remember getting in her car and then waking up in my bed, head pounding, mouth dry, with a terrible sense that I had done something awful.

*Drinker's remorse,* I thought as I caught sight of the clock. *Too early to be awake.*

I woke up again at ten to the sound of the doorbell. I stumbled out of bed and found Chloe at my door.

"Morning, kiddo," she said with a grin.

"Don't call me kiddo," I grumbled at her. "I'm older than you."

"I have a plan," she told me as she squeezed past me, into my house.

"A plan for what?" I held a hand to my pounding head and followed her into the kitchen.

"To get Vanessa, of course."

That woke me up. How did Chloe know that I wanted Vanessa? "To what?"

"Get Vanessa. You know, the woman you're in love with. The woman you want to submit to."

"How the hell do you know that?"

"You don't remember the drive home, do you?" Chloe smirked. "Kiddo, you told me everything. Now, here's my plan…"

\* \* \*

My whole body shook as I lowered myself to my knees. Chloe had hold of the leash that was attached to my collar. I kept my eyes to the ground, half terrified that I would spot Vanessa when she walked into the room, half scared that she wouldn't turn up.

*It's just a small party,* I reassured myself. *You know almost everyone here.*

But wasn't that worse? I could hear people asking if that was Lily at Chloe's feet. I could feel people staring at us, imagine them wondering what the hell was going on. Chloe had thought that it would be easier to go to a small, private party, rather than a big club. I had agreed at the time. I wasn't so sure now.

I couldn't concentrate on the conversation that Chloe was having with one of our acquaintances. My heart pounded like a drum in my chest, drowning out everything else. When would Vanessa get there? What would she say? Would she even care? What if she was indifferent?

"What the fuck is going on?"

My eyes darted up at the sound of Vanessa's voice. She wasn't looking at me. Her question was directed at Chloe.

"What do you mean? I'm having a drink with Louise."

"Why is Lily on a leash? Did she lose a bet?"

I could feel my face heating up and I let my gaze drop to the floor. I was sure everyone must be staring at us now.

"She's on a leash because she's submissive," Chloe said calmly.

"She's not a submissive. She's a Domme. She's always been a Domme."

"She looks pretty submissive to me," Chloe said.

"She doesn't even switch," Vanessa shot back.

My breath caught, and I waited in expectation of what she would say next.

"This is wrong," Vanessa said. "This is completely fucked up, that's what this is. She's wrong."

It felt like my heart shattered in my chest. I wanted to run, I wanted to cry. I couldn't do either. I kept my head low but I could see her boots turn and walk the other way.

"Shall we go?" Chloe asked me.

I nodded, sure that if I tried to talk the tears would escape. I tried not to make eye contact with anyone as I followed Chloe out of the room. I unclipped the leash as soon as we were away from prying eyes, gave her back the collar and found my coat under the mountain that had built up at the bottom of the stairs.

"Are you okay?" Chloe asked.

"I'll be fine," I told her.

"I can drive you home, if you want."

I shook my head. "It's a five-minute walk."

"She probably needs some time."

"Maybe," I said but I knew it wasn't true. I had been right before. Vanessa didn't care about me.

\* \* \*

I ignored everyone's calls. I was done with the lifestyle and everyone I knew in it. I would reinvent myself. There was a whole queer scene that didn't involve bondage, discipline and domination. I could become a part of that, make new friends. I could hang out in bars that didn't have spanking benches. After I was done sitting in my house sobbing, that is.

Vanessa hadn't called. Not once. Not even a text message.

Five years of friendship and it was over, just like that.

*This is completely fucked up.*

Every time I thought that I was somewhere close to being okay again I would remember her words.

*She's wrong.* Her words tormented me, slipping into my consciousness whenever I wasn't distracting myself. What had I done to deserve such harsh words? We were friends. If nothing else, we had been friends.

I woke Sunday morning to a text message she'd sent in the early hours.

*Why aren't you at the club?*

My resolve to ignore her message lasted for all of half an hour before I messaged back.

*Fuck off, Vanessa.*

For a moment I felt happy with my response. She'd been a bitch. She'd humiliated me in front of everyone we knew. I didn't owe her an explanation as to why I wasn't in the club. Did she expect things to just go back to normal?

Was she expecting me to keep pretending? Well, fuck that because I was done with it. I would rather join the vanilla world than go back to watching Vanessa dominate every sub who wasn't me.

By midday the satisfaction faded and I was back to feeling like shit. I wanted to ignore whoever was knocking on my door. I'd ignored the doorbell but now it seemed like whoever was out there was trying to break the door down.

"Lily," Vanessa's voice came through the letterbox. "Lily, open the door."

I shot to my feet, my heart suddenly reanimated and pounding in my chest.

*Today would have been a good day to reacquaint yourself with make up.*

I ran a hand through the mass of blonde curls that I hadn't bothered to tame that day and hoped that my face didn't look as puffy as it had earlier.

She stood on the other side of my door, looking like hell but still just as perfect to me as ever. Her eyes were bloodshot, rimmed with dark circles.

"Can I come in?" she asked.

I shook my head. "What do you want?"

"I want to talk to you."

"I don't have anything to say."

"Then just listen to me. Please, let me in. I don't want to have this conversation out here."

I stepped back reluctantly, not wanting to hear what she had to say but wanting my neighbours to hear it even less.

I followed her into the living room. She gestured to the seat on the sofa next to her and I sat down.

"I'm sorry for my reaction," she said. "I wasn't expecting to see you there, like that, with Chloe."

"It's okay," I said, not because it was okay but because that's what you say when someone apologises.

"I thought that we were closer than that," Vanessa

continued. "Why didn't you tell me?"

"I was scared of how you'd react," I told her honestly. "I guess I knew it would ruin everything."

"I just don't understand. You've been dominant for years…"

"I've never been a Domme, not really."

"Then why pretend?"

"Imagine how you would feel on the other side. Imagine being the one on the receiving end. It's scary, it's—" I shook my head and stopped talking. She would never understand. There was no point explaining.

When I didn't continue, Vanessa said, "But it's been years. You've been acting this way for years. All those subs we shared… Why?"

"I can't explain it. Anyway, it's over now. I'm not going to go back to how things were."

"Do you love her?"

"Who?" I frowned at her.

"Chloe."

"Chloe? Oh," I said as realisation dawned. "Chloe and I, we aren't involved or anything."

"You aren't?"

I shook my head. "She was just helping me to… come out, I guess."

"You're not sleeping with her?"

"No."

"You were wearing her collar."

"I was wearing *a* collar."

"You were kneeling at her feet," she accused.

"Submissives aren't allowed on the furniture," I reminded her.

She seemed to be taking a minute to process what had been said. I stared at my hands, wishing I had a way to break the awkward silence. It had never been awkward between us before. I guessed things were different, now that I wasn't a Domme. If life had felt empty when I was just her friend, what was it going to feel like when I was nothing at all to her?

"You aren't involved with Chloe?" she finally asked.

"She's just my friend."

"Will you come with me to the Red Room on Thursday?"

We always went to the monthly lesbian S&M night together. But hadn't she been listening to me? "I'm done with acting dominant, Vanessa. I'm not—"

"As my submissive," she interrupted. "I want you to come with me as my submissive."

"Oh." I felt my face heat up, my mouth turn upwards involuntarily. "Yes, that would be nice."

"I can promise you that nice will not be the way you describe it on Friday morning."

"Really?" My stomach tied itself in knots.

Vanessa gave me the evil grin that I had seen directed at so many other women. "Don't be scared. I'll take good care of you."

She leaned forward and brushed her lips over mine. The kiss was over before I had a chance to respond. Sweet and chaste and nothing like the kisses we had shared in the past.

"I don't ever want to see you on the end of Chloe's leash again. Do you understand?"

I nodded.

"Or kneeling at her feet. In fact, I would prefer that you don't ever talk to her again."

I rolled my eyes. "She's my friend and she's your friend too."

"Was my friend," Vanessa corrected.

"Don't be like that. She was trying to help me."

"She was trying to steal you."

"I promise not to let her put me on a leash and not to kneel at her feet if you promise not to ruin your friendship with her over something silly."

"It's not silly," Vanessa said. "But I promise. I'll see you on Thursday."

\* \* \*

The Red Room was still quiet when we arrived. I was grateful for that. I needed some time to compose myself before I faced my friends. I was wearing a tiny leather skirt and a red corset that Vanessa had picked out for me. I could barely walk in the heels she had insisted on and it was a relief when she took our drinks and headed for the seating area.

"Kneel," she told me as she took a seat on the sofa.

I knelt down in front of her, my mind all over the place. What did she intend to do tonight? Were we going to play or would we just watch? What would happen when our friends saw us? Some of them hadn't been at the party and they wouldn't know that I was submissive. Why had Vanessa asked me to come here with her? Because she was interested in me as a submissive or because she owed it to years of friendship?

"How are you feeling?" Vanessa asked.

"Nervous," I said. "I haven't seen anyone since the party."

She stroked my hair, tangled her hand gently in it. "Don't worry about them. You aren't here for them."

I gave her a shaky smile. I wasn't there for them, I was there for her.

"I want a foot rub," Vanessa said.

"From me?"

Vanessa smiled. "Of course, from you."

She slipped her foot out of her shoe. I shuffled back so that she could place it comfortably in my hands and began to rub. She had beautiful feet. Smooth and soft and perfectly pedicured. Vanessa let out a sigh as I pressed firmly on the sole of her foot and rubbed. I wanted to kiss them but she hadn't told me to and I didn't want to do anything wrong. After a few minutes everything else drifted away. I forgot about my anxieties. There was no one to think about but Vanessa, nothing to worry about but pleasing her.

"Use your mouth," Vanessa said after a while.

It was all the encouragement I needed. I lifted her foot higher and sucked one of her toes into my mouth, swirling my tongue around. I trailed kisses up her foot and to her ankle. I kissed my way back down her foot and took each toe into my mouth. I closed my eyes as a perfect sense of peace came over me. I was finally where I needed to be, finally where I belonged.

"May we join you?"

My eyes shot open as Chloe's voice interrupted my moment of serenity. I sat upright, letting Vanessa's toe slip from my mouth.

"There are other seats available," Vanessa said coldly.

"I want to sit here. Vicky, kneel."

Chloe sat down next to Vanessa and her submissive lowered herself gracefully beside me.

"I didn't tell you to stop," Vanessa said to me.

I began to massage her foot again, my eyes remaining on her, waiting to see what would happen.

"Are you going to LAM on Sunday?" Chloe asked.

"I don't know," Vanessa said.

"I would like a new corset before the summer party," Chloe continued. "I wish I had bought that one we saw last month."

"Excuse us please, Chloe, apparently my submissive doesn't know how to follow orders."

My heart jumped into my throat as Vanessa stood and held a hand out to me. I took her hand and allowed her to help me to my feet. She held on to my hand as we walked across the club, towards the backroom. The room was half empty at that time of the night. There was a submissive in a cage, being taunted by her Dommes, and a few others tied up around the room. The crowds hadn't yet gathered. That was something. The backroom had never seemed so intimidating from the other side.

We reached the back wall and Vanessa pushed me to my knees. She wound a hand through my hair and tugged hard enough to hurt. I looked up at her, feeling equal parts terrified and exhilarated.

"I told you not to stop."

"I'm sorry."

"When we're in this kind of setting I expect obedience. You may use your safe word but you may not disobey me. Especially not in front of Chloe."

"I'm sorry," I apologised again, realising that this was part of the game, that this was part of being Vanessa's submissive for the evening.

"We're going to use a traffic light system. If you need me to slow down you say orange, if you need me to stop you say red. Do you understand?"

"Yes."

She tugged on my hair. "Yes, who?"

"Yes, Mistress."

"I want you to use them if you need to. I won't be disappointed."

I nodded. "What are *you* going to use?"

She paused for a moment. In her position, as I had been many times, I wouldn't have told but it was my first time and perhaps that was why she told me.

"I'm just going to use a paddle."

I took a deep breath as panic threatened to take over. I was going to let her paddle me. I had fantasised about it for so long but the reality was more terrifying than I had anticipated. It was going to hurt.

"I'm scared," I said.

She tugged me to my feet and pulled me towards her. She wound her arms around my waist and kissed me.

"It will be fine, I promise. If you don't want to do this

we don't have to."

"I do want to."

She kissed me again, this time harder, letting her tongue invade my mouth. When she pulled back she ordered me to remove my skirt. I removed it and handed it to her.

"Turn around."

I turned. She unlaced my corset and let it fall to the floor. I had been naked in front of her and half of the club dozens of times but I hadn't felt vulnerable before. Vanessa took my hand and walked me to the wall where two shackles hung. She took one of my arms and secured it to the wall and then did the same to the other.

She brushed my hair away from my shoulder and leaned forward so that her lips grazed my ear as she said, "I want you to feel this when you wake up tomorrow morning and think of me. I want you to think of me when you see the bruises in the mirror and every time it hurts to sit down."

My breath caught in anticipation and all my worries flew away. This was what I wanted. Vanessa's complete attention, her discipline, her pain.

She slipped a blindfold over my eyes and for a second I could feel the panic building in my chest. Vanessa ran a hand down my back and over my bum, soothing my anxiety, reminding me whom I was there to serve. Then the contact was broken and I waited in anticipation of the first strike.

"Count," she ordered as she brought the paddle down on my arse cheeks.

"One," I cried out as pain warmed my arse. "Two. Three. Four. Five," I whimpered as the pain seemed to spread, to consume the entire area.

"Six. Seven. Eight. Nine. Ten. Eleven."

My voice sounded further away, the pain dulled now. I floated, blissfully unaware of everything except the paddle and then Vanessa's hands tracing the path where the paddle had been. Vanessa's voice telling me how well I had taken my punishment, how good I was.

She pulled the blindfold from my eyes and released my arms. I felt my legs wobble. Her arms wound around my waist and I leaned back against her, closing my eyes to block out the lights, dim though they were.

"You were perfect," she said.

She brushed her lips against my neck, flicked her tongue out against my pulse and then bit down gently.

"You make me want to mark you so that everyone will know that you're mine."

"You don't need to mark me to make me yours."

She led me to a chair nearby and sat down, pulling me onto her lap. I curled up against her, satisfied in a way that I never felt after sex.

She ran a hand over my hair and pushed my head back before claiming my mouth in a kiss. Her hand found my nipple and she rolled it gently between her fingers. My nipple hardened and my pussy hummed with arousal. Her other hand brushed over my pussy. Her touch was soft but my body felt so sensitive. I pushed my hips up, whimpered into her mouth, needing her to touch me, to make me come.

She pulled back from the kiss, released my nipple and placed both of her hands on my hips.

"Let's get you dressed and head home."

"Home?"

I tried to think past the fog that lingered in my brain, through the arousal that wouldn't go away.

"Have I done something wrong?"

The thought that I had somehow displeased her made my heart clench.

"No, you've been perfect," she assured me. "But I need to fuck you and there's no sex allowed here."

She caught my mouth again in a kiss before allowing me to climb to my feet and helping me back into my clothes. She took my hand and I followed her out of the club, barely noticing our mutual friends as we passed them. In that moment she was everything and nothing and no one else mattered.

\* \* \*

She had me pinned against the wall before the front door to her flat had even clicked closed. She held my arms against my sides as her mouth devoured mine. She used her knee to push my legs open, exposing my bare pussy.

"Don't move your arms," she ordered. I left them where they were. She ran a finger over my clitoris and down further, sliding it into my wetness. I pushed forward, wanting more. She slapped my thigh.

"You're not in charge here. Stay still."

She ran her thumb over my clit and a small ripple of pleasure went through me.

"Please, Vanessa."

"Oh sweetie, beg if you want, but it won't change anything."

She withdrew her finger. A smile played on her lips, the cold smile I had seen directed at so many other subs. This wasn't Vanessa my friend, this wasn't the indulgent Domme from the club, this was Vanessa the sadist.

"What's your safe word?"

"Red."

"Good. Use it if you need to. Get on your knees, bitch."

I sunk down to my knees and she took hold of my hair, pulling it tightly. My eyes watered but I wanted more. I wanted everything she had to give. I wanted to be the sub who could take everything she had to give. The sub she didn't have to hold back with.

"Follow me. Don't stand."

I crawled behind her into the bedroom.

"Stay."

I did as I was ordered, stopping in the middle of her

room, next to her bed.

I could hear her open her wardrobe behind me and take things out. I held my breath as I heard her walking towards me. She unlaced my corset before moving in front of me. It was then that I saw the nipple clamps. I forced myself to stay still as the fear heightened my arousal.

"Do you need to use your safe word?"

I shook my head. "No, Mistress."

She pinched my right nipple between her fingers until it was erect enough to attach the clamp to. As she let the clamp close around my nipple I let out a hiss of pain.

"Don't hold back," Vanessa said. "I want to hear your pain, I want to see it."

She lowered her mouth to my other nipple and sucked it into her mouth before biting down. I cried out, the pain sending a jolt of pleasure to my pussy. She attached the clamp and I knew that the pain was nothing compared to how it would feel when she removed it. I'd done this to women countless times but the tiny thrill I got from hurting them was nothing compared to how it felt to submit to Vanessa's pain.

"Put your hands behind your back."

I resisted the urge to turn and watch her as she walked behind me and I put my hands behind my back. A moment later I felt rough rope around my wrists as Vanessa secured my hands. I wiggled them when she was done, but they were tied tightly.

"You're not getting out of those until I let you."

I watched as Vanessa unbuttoned her leather trousers. She turned her back to me as she lowered them, revealing her perfect arse. She stepped out of her shoes and pushed her trousers further down before stepping out of them too. She pulled her top over her head and threw it across the bed. She looked over her shoulder at me as she slowly pushed her thong down off of her hips and let it drop to the floor. She kicked it off and turned towards me, her pussy right there in front of my eager mouth.

"Tell me what you want."

"I want to lick your pussy."

"How selfless." Her tone was mocking. "Is that all you want?"

I shook my head. "I want you to lick me too. I want you to fuck me."

"With what?"

"Whatever you want."

She pushed my head towards her and ordered me to lick. She kept her hands on my head, holding me firmly in place as I licked and sucked her to orgasm.

"Open your legs. I want to see your cunt."

I spread my legs, the tiny skirt bunching around my waist as I did so. Vanessa slid her foot along one of my thighs and up towards my pussy. She rubbed her toe over my clit, back and forth, over and over as I felt my orgasm building.

"Can I come? Please, Mistress."

"Yes. Come."

The pleasure overtook me the minute I had her permission. I sagged forward, drained from my orgasm, but she wasn't finished with me. She knelt on the floor in front of me.

"Take a deep breath, pet."

I did as she said just as she released one of my nipple clamps. The small bite of pain when the clamp had been applied was nothing compared to the agony I felt as the blood rushed back. Vanessa bent her head to my breast and gently sucked the nipple into her mouth, running her tongue over it until the pain subsided.

"Are you okay?" she asked as she wiped the tears from my cheek.

"It hurt," I said.

"I know, but you look so beautiful when you're in pain. I have to remove the other one."

I nodded and tried to blink away the tears.

"Tell me when you're ready, pet."

"I'm ready. Just get it over with."

This time I screamed out as she removed the clamp, her mouth replacing it a second later, her tongue soothing me.

She untied my arms and sat on the bed. She held a hand out to me. "Come here."

I took her hand, stood and allowed her to pull me onto her lap. I wrapped my legs around her waist as she kissed me. She reached down between our bodies and slid two fingers into me.

"You took my pain so well," she said as she rubbed her thumb over my clit.

"I liked it," I told her.

"I can tell." She added a third finger.

"Please let me come," I asked as I felt the orgasm building again.

"Not yet."

"Please, Mistress," I wasn't sure I could hold on.

"You'll come when I'm ready."

She withdrew her fingers.

"On your back, on the bed. Spread your legs."

I obeyed her orders, letting my knees fall open. She crawled up on the bed towards me and then her mouth was on my pussy, her tongue flicking out over my clit, her teeth gently scraping, the bite of pain enough to send me over the edge. I couldn't hide the stolen orgasm from her. The smile on her face suggested that she had intended for it to happen.

"Time for another punishment, pet."

∗ ∗ ∗

I woke late the next morning in Vanessa's bed. My body was sore but I was happier than I could remember being.

"Morning," Vanessa said with a smile.

"Morning," I replied with a smile of my own.

She brushed her lips over mine.

"How are you feeling today?"

"Good," I replied.

"Not too tender?"

"I feel perfectly sore."

She laughed. "You're perfect for me, you know."

"I know. You should probably thank Chloe."

"Don't ever say her name in our bed again," she said, but she was smiling.

"If it wasn't for her this never would have happened."

"If you had come to me instead of her... Why did you tell her? If you couldn't tell me..."

"I was drunk."

"You've been drunk with me."

"It's different."

"How?"

"I'm not..." *In love with her.* "...attracted to Chloe."

Vanessa rolled on top of me, pinning me to the bed.

"Good. Because I'm keeping you and I don't intend to share you."

"You used to share your submissives with me," I reminded her. I tried to keep my tone nonchalant but I wanted to scream that I wanted monogamy, that I didn't want to share her any more than she wanted to share me.

"I don't need to share submissives with you now that you are submissive. We don't need anyone else."

"Really?" I asked hopefully.

"Really. I love you. You know that, right?"

I shook my head. "I didn't know that."

"I've always loved you. Even when I thought you were a Domme."

"I love you too."

Vanessa smiled down at me. "You're mine now."

And she was, and is, my everything.

# INSIDE
### LEANDRA VANE

I've had my eyes on the redhead at the end of the third row all night.

From the moment she entered the room I could see she was all business. Dressed entirely in black with a purpose behind every movement of her body. She wore sharp-toed boots and a silky blouse that hung in a low, luscious V. When the gallery opened, the woman had not mingled, had not meandered about the canvases or weaved around the sculptures. She had not even given the cheese plates and wine a single glance. She simply snagged a brochure listing the artists in residency and glided to the end of the third row. She clamped the brakes on her sleek, sporty wheelchair and waited for the presentation to begin.

I had a distinct impression she was refusing to look at any of the pieces until she had heard what the artists had to say. As one of the presenting artists myself this was, shall we say, unnerving as fuck. Whatever happened to letting art speak for itself? This woman's approach was completely backward and made me feel utterly exposed. Feeling myself becoming obsessed, I rushed over to indulge in the wine and cheese, with an emphasis on the wine.

I was fairly warm by the time the gallery director wrangled the audience into seats and the artists toward the podium to begin our presentations. I wasn't speaking first, so I had some time to simmer in my anxious anticipation.

The gallery was kept cool to combat the heat of the spotlights and the intimate mix of patrons. Usually the crisp scent of canvas tinged with the edge of oils was refreshing and soothing, but all I felt was tension tethered by the woman's intense gaze. She shifted as the artists began to speak, taking in each and every word.

She had a fine gold chain around her neck and she toyed with it using her index finger while tracing along her collarbone with the tip of her pinky. A line of sweat pricked along the back of my neck. I was thankful to have just had my hair cut, but the taffy I used to spike it up felt heavy about my crown. I was practically suffocating here.

Now, look. It's not often I get crushes at first sight, but... but... *damn.* Perhaps she was some big time critic or lofty collector, but she could have told me she taught finger-painting to kindergarteners and I would have still craved even a shred of her approval. The angle of her wrist as she rested her chin on her knuckles pointed to the fact that she was above finger-painting, though. She was waiting to be impressed.

The second artist began his speech. He was a funny guy, so the audience laughed. A low rumble that vibrated in my gut. The woman allowed only the faintest crescent of a smile to part her lips.

I pulled a couple of index cards from my back pocket. I hadn't planned on needing notes to explain pieces I had been working on for years, but then an art affectionate reincarnation of Rita Hayworth landed in the third row and made me drink three glasses of wine.

Giving my lip ring a nibble, I looked down at my shoes. Bright pink pumps that clashed ferociously with my mustard corduroy pants and were far too dressy for the loose baseball tee that hung on my Flapper frame. This was the first time I ever reconsidered my ironic punky artist image and wished I owned at least one nice skirt. The tips of my shoes pointed together like an apology.

Inevitably, my turn arrived and I took the stand.

I shoved all my panicked thoughts about looking like a scrubby teenager to the back of my mind and anchored myself by the heels of my shoes. I read off my cards.

I'm sure there were some intelligent ideas written on

them, but in my own head I only heard nonsense. *Art. I make that. See those canvases over there with the things stuck on them? I arted those. I art a lot. I like collage. Something something Hannah Höch. She arted too. Photomontage. Art is nice. The end.*

Fuck.

I was back in my seat, knees trembling, before the spattering of applause for my spiel had dissipated. The next resident took over and my muscles relaxed as the woman's attention moved along with the program.

Somehow I managed to make it through the rest of the presentations without squirming out of my chair. Her pinky never left her collarbone. I commanded myself not to dive for the wine and decided I would stroll over to my canvases as the crowd dispersed and make the best of whatever happened.

What happened was the woman made it to my canvas before I did. Of all the pieces in the place she chose mine first, and without even a moment's hesitation. There was nothing written on my note cards that would help me now. I had been given a chance and I had to take it. Fuck strolling. I threw my shoulders back and I strutted right up to my provocative patron.

"Good evening," I said, with a professional flourish. "I'm Delilah Max."

"Valerie Adams." She did not offer to shake my hand, just stared full on at my canvas. "You are from St. Louis?"

My heart sank. I had fibbed in my bio. I was from a suburb of St. Louis. All right, not really a suburb. A small town about forty miles from St. Louis. A backwoods Missouri hick town. Not St. Louis.

"Yes."

"Do you like being so far from home?"

I didn't. "Being in Seattle is very exciting."

"You have interesting work."

*Score.* "Thank you."

"But your message seems hollow."

*Shit.* "Is collage of particular interest to you?"

"That should not matter."

*Of course not.* "Well... I've always let my work speak for itself. I think too many artists get in the way of the art."

"And when should I be expecting something to come at me in this canvas?"

My silence served as an answer.

"One can forgive a student for being superfluous on message and shallow on skill, but when the practicing artist is high on technique but low on perspective, well, that certainly is sticky."

*Sticky?* This was not going well. My sexual Siren had lured me in and now she was eating me alive.

Valerie brushed a burgundy lock behind her ear. "Well, then. What *inspires* you?"

I jumped on the opportunity to redeem myself.

"I'm really interested in texture and how that reflects a larger social metaphor... For example, the low quality of the paper the coupons are printed on contrasts with the vintage wallpaper—"

"Yes, yes, you have texture down," she interrupted, "but you lack focus."

My jaw clenched, but I transferred the tension to my fists so I could speak.

"The eye is drawn up to the horizon here—"

"That isn't what I mean. Focus is not on the surface. I see your horizons, I see your center of focus, your subtle sense of balance. That's what got you here. What I can't see is what is inside."

"In... side."

"Yes, inside. You need to get *inside* this work, or this will be the end of the line for your career."

Immersed in my insecurity I used the shards of my broken heart to fight back.

"All right, I need to *get inside*... Are you saying you're some sort of expert in that department?"

"I am."

I jiggled my lip ring. "How so?"

Valerie didn't miss a beat. "I'm a Domme."

I'm not sure what I was expecting but it wasn't that.

"Domme," I repeated, dumb and numb.

"As in, Dominant. Dominatrix, if you wish. And I can spot a pickup line when I hear one." She shifted toward me, smiling for the first time. "If you're surprised you should know Seattle is known for this sort of thing."

"I am aware." My brain cycled through pop culture references and a few snippets of articles I had read late at night that I had deleted from my browsing history. I was miserably unaware. "But I'm not interested." *So, there.*

"Really."

"Really. I'm not the type that gets turned on by being told what to do." The child inside me decided since she had been so quick to criticize my work then I was entitled to criticize her Dommely-Dommeliness. "Besides, you say it like it's such a serious thing. *Domme.* The word itself sounds like the ding of a clumsy church bell. It doesn't exactly make me want to get on my knees and lick some boots."

"I can also spot a dare when I hear one."

My stomach lurched. "Are… are we going to talk about art anymore, or are we finished here?"

"That's up to you."

"How… so?"

"A linguist you are not, but there is some hope for your art."

My face flushed with frustration. Her cryptic criticism was pissing me off but I was also enchanted by the hint that she might actually sort of like my work. That and this Valerie Adams smelled very good. Like coconut and sugar cookies all at once. *Wait, wait, wait. Domme. Shit.*

"And improving my art has something to do with… Domination?"

"Perhaps. If you are willing."

"I am willing, but I already told you I am not interested."

"Hm. We shall see." With a flick of her wrist she steered her chair around and whisked herself away.

I followed her.

She led us down a side corridor and I looked over my shoulder, nervous someone would be curious as to where we were going. I had to run to catch up as she tapped the automatic door opener mounted on the wall and pushed out into the courtyard.

The center had an impressive patio that was nearly a park in itself. There were places for grilling and plenty of benches and furniture dispersed through a paved maze of hedges and small trees in decorative pots. We rounded the large, bubbling fountain in the center of the compound and ventured further down a narrow, unlit path.

The August evening was quickly cooling. It was nearly ten o'clock and a mistiness hung in the air that reminded me of spring mornings back home. I couldn't believe summer was down to its last thread.

Valerie jetted silently in front of me and the tapping of my heels were the only sound in the dark. I forced myself to walk ahead with confidence as my eyes adjusted to the night.

We ended in a cul-de-sac where the path formed a circle around a single patch of grass. We were granted privacy by the tall, manicured hedge. It was very dark, and very quiet. Valerie began a slow lap around the circle.

"For being so disinterested you certainly had no problems keeping up."

I shook my head to slow the rush of emotions throbbing at my temples.

"You called my bluff. But, really, if you hate my work so much, why did you drag me out here?"

"Oh, dear, I don't hate your art, and I didn't drag you anywhere. If you didn't want to be out here, you wouldn't be."

"So, what gives?"

"What *gives* is that you have fight but no claws. I wanted to talk to you because of all the personalities poured into oils and resin and pulp in that gallery, yours is the only one that resonated on more than a superficial level. But there's something missing. You need help, and I think I might just have the power to nudge you along. I don't do this for just anyone."

"You don't, huh? And here I thought I was going to be the one serving you."

"We'll get to that."

My heart skipped into a faster pace.

"Shouldn't we have like, negotiations and safe words, and… stuff like that?"

"You may choose a safe word if you would like, but I don't think it is necessary."

A list of artists scrolled through my brain and for some reason I spit out, "Francisco Goya".

"Goya? Ick. How about Gentileschi, or at least Matisse?"

I let out a deep breath. "Kahlo."

"Deal. But I don't think you'll need it."

"Why won't I?"

"Because I'm not going to touch you. If you want to do the things I ask of you, you will. If you don't, you won't. Simple."

"Simple." I let out a hot huff. "What would you like me to do?"

"Take off your shirt."

My heart thudded three even beats. So, this was where she was going with this. Push me to the edge, make me take a risk. I shrugged. I paid for an entire semester of my undergrad as a nude model for a sketcher's night class. I pulled the tee over my head and tossed it toward her.

"Step out of your shoes."

I kicked them to the side with attitude, but the cold

concrete flush against my bare skin made me squeak.

"Yes, it's a bit cold, but you won't die. Now your pants, and underthings."

*And underthings.* I obeyed with quick motions, breathing against the bite of the cold air in intimate places.

A pale outline of Valerie's figure was all I could make out in the dark. The line of her cheek, the curve of her hand resting on her left wheel. I wondered what parts of my naked body she could make out, if she saw the contours of my hips, the dark patch of hair between my legs, or the glints of metal rings in my rock hard nipples. I remained still, my arms at my side.

"Very well. Walk to the middle of the circle. The grass will feel nice, I'm certain."

The grass did not feel nice. It was actually quite pokey and scratchy on my feet, but her next words revealed why she wanted me off the cement.

"Now kneel."

I lowered myself to the ground, running my fingers through the cold grass.

"Get down on both knees. Lower your head. Lower your shoulders. Further. *Tighter.*"

I hunched down as far as I could, resting my head on my forearms. My ass was stuck in the air and I couldn't believe I was in such a derogatory state. Until I remembered I put myself in it.

"Now, close your eyes and imagine…" There was a pause and when she spoke again her voice came from my other side. Valerie was circling around me. "Imagine what I could do to you in such a position."

My mind exploded with possibilities with an ease that frightened me and for a moment I forgot where I was. I brought myself back, picking at the grass. She noticed my squirming.

"Don't move."

A surge of guilt stilled my fidgeting.

"What did you imagine, hm? Did my hands cup your breasts? Did my teeth graze the back of your neck? Or perhaps I took advantage of your submissive stance and ran my fingertips slick against your wet pussy, toying with your clit, dipping my fingers inside?"

I was breathless, the cold sinking in, heat rising. I had imagined all those things.

"Do I fuck you hard or do I lick you slowly, lovingly? Do I pull your hair or do I caress your curves and tease your nipples? Do they plump and pulse between my lips? Do we kiss, Delilah? Or do you crawl to me and beg me to take you over my knee and show you where you've gone wrong?"

I took in each suggestion wilder than the next, each more sweet, each more enticing than the next. Yes, I wanted her domination, I wanted her to take me, to shake me, to punish me. I wanted to give that part of myself to her for her to handle however she knew was best.

"Tell me."

My lips were parted, my tongue daring to release the request and when I finally gave in, my voice held the tone of a plea. "I want you to spank me."

A crack popped behind me and I gasped.

She had—but she couldn't have. I felt a blossom of pain, a jerk of my body against the impact, and a swell of desire for more. But she had not touched me. In the next moment a clap popped off in front of me. I imagined her firm hand and my awaiting flesh beneath her rule. I moaned.

"Again," I implored.

*Crack.*

"Again."

"Now, now. Ask nicely."

An ache stretched between my legs.

"Please… please, again."

Another slap echoed in the night. I rocked forward, my toes curling and my ankles tense. I let out another gasping moan.

"Yes, thank you. Thank you."

"Touch yourself, Delilah. For me."

I plunged my hand between my legs and began to soothe the agony of want with my fingertips. I stroked my vulva with three firm fingers, rubbing the searing pleasure as hard as I could. I wanted to scream. I wanted to feel the weight of my breasts against her lap, to feel the force of surrender, the unrelenting rhythm of release.

There was one more pop in the dark, a clip of surprise and I was gone. Orgasm shot up my spine and I came undone. I felt like all the little pieces of myself I had been trying to hold in, tight, secret, suddenly cascaded to the ground like an upset jar of marbles. A million pieces of my soul scattered like the stars in the night sky. In that moment I saw all my deepest fears and felt all my deepest shames and floated in a weightless realization that I had managed to let it all go.

When I surfaced I was clutching a fistful of grass and had tears in the corners of my eyes. Valerie's voice was soft when she spoke.

"There. Now, why don't you get dressed and warmed up before we go back to the party."

I crawled to my pile of clothes and fumbled like a toddler in a Halloween costume to get put back together. As I dressed myself, I noticed for the first time how well my clothes conformed to the shape of my body, returning me to the comfort and security of my own skin. All the defensiveness of my image seemed to be melting and my clothes enveloped me in a simple kind of contentment. I looked up at her in the dark.

"Come here. I can hold you if you would like?"

I sniffed. "I would."

"You can sit on my lap, here."

Climbing into her she was so soft, with curves I had neglected to notice beyond her calculated demeanor in the gallery. Her rounded cheek rested gently on my forehead.

Before I could stop myself my confession bubbled from my lips.

"My name isn't Delilah Max. It's Deana Maxwell. And I'm not from St. Louis. I graduated from a state college in the middle of nowhere in Missouri and I have no idea what I'm going to do with my art career after this residency is over."

She caressed the side of my face and pulled me into her embrace. "You will make more art and go places you haven't even dreamed of yet. You have skill, talent, and a perspective—when it breaks through, you'll be unstoppable."

I buried my face in her silkiness, just above her breasts. "Is that your version of telling me *good girl?*"

"Perhaps. I'm not sure you're quite ready to appreciate those words just yet."

A few moments of silence passed and I built up the nerve to finally ask, "Are you seeing... er, uh... Dominating anyone right now?"

"That's a conversation to be had when you are in an entirely different head space. Perhaps over coffee. I read you are scheduled to be here for another five weeks, so there will be time for that." I felt her body stiffen, then relax. "But the answer is no. Not right now."

We sat beneath the cold night with each other for several minutes.

"I like your shoes," she said, breaking the silence. "Perhaps you will leave them on next time."

I dared a mischievous tone. "Will next time be soon?"

"I hope so. If I can do that to you just by talking, I am interested to see what will happen if you let me set my hands on you."

"Oh... I have an idea."

"I'm sure you do. But first, let's go back in. I have a few things to add to our lesson, and it includes a discussion of that horrid wallpaper in your piece. Are you ready?"

I nodded. I slipped off her warm body and stretched

my rejuvenated muscles. As we made our way back to the gallery, the heels of my shoes tapped with an echo I had never before noticed. I was ready to work. I was ready to break down and rebuild. I was, finally, ready to get inside.

# VEGAS MISTRESS
## SAMANTHA LUCE

*What happens in Vegas… when you never want to leave?*

Anticipation. Carly Simon wrote a song about it. She knows my struggle as I sit cross-legged on the small white sofa with the garish red pillows. I've been doing so much anticipating in the past couple of months. This trip should have only lasted two weeks. For two weeks I could go without a visit to Lady Victoria's *Pit*. I could satisfy my own needs or just deny them. Denial is one of the best aphrodisiacs I've discovered. The longer I go, the greater the reward when at last I am allowed the sweet release.

Nine weeks though, that is a bit much. Especially since that period of time has been chock full of mergers, take-overs, acquisitions, and terminations. If I have to look at another spreadsheet or PowerPoint presentation I think I might just go postal. At this moment, sitting with my back rigid and my hands folded demurely on my lap, I am a bundle of heightened nerves laying on a bed of unstable dynamite that could ignite at any moment. I shift my legs, hoping to feel the thrill of my panties tightening over my pussy. I've been performing this move repeatedly during these last few weeks. It was barely enough at first. Now, it has completely lost its powers. I am too far gone.

Aside from the sofa I am seated on, the only other furnishing is a foot long rectangular clock with large neon numbers. It is one minute from the witching hour. I have been wavering between watching the clock and the two doors. The plain door I originally entered just ten minutes ago, which could allow me a coward's escape. Or the ornately carved door across from me, behind which should be my new mistress and God only knows what sorts of games and pleasures.

Three things happen almost at once. The numbers on the clock turn from 11:59 to 12:00. The door full of promise snicks open. All light is extinguished. It is so dark I lift my hand and cannot see it. I hear the click and clack of my mistress's heels on the tile floor. My breath catches.

"Don't move." A commanding voice near my left ear. I am unable to catch it right then with just two words spoken, but later I will fall in absolute lust with her regal British accent.

The total darkness, anxiousness over what is to come, and her nearness have my heart thundering at a rapid pace. My breaths have become shallow and quick. There's a hint of spice and leather in the air.

She collects my hair in her hand and draws it forward over my right shoulder. Warm minty-fresh breath teases the hairs on the back of my neck. "You have already committed one punishable infraction by being on the furniture without permission.

My faux pas shames me. I start to get up. Her soft hands grip my shoulders firmly. "I just told you not to move. That's two infractions. Keep track of them."

At that moment I am torn. I want to answer and tell her yes, Mistress, but she has not given me permission to speak. Nodding would mean more movement. I do not want to risk displeasing her any more during the first minutes of our meeting.

Her hands come around and she begins unfastening the buttons on my silk blouse. "I have spoken with your mistress, Lady Victoria," she says in that soft, fancy voice of hers as she continues to slowly unveil me. "I know everything you crave the most. Once I have granted you permission to speak you will address me as Mistress or Lady M. Any deviation will result in more punishment." On the last word she pinches both my nipples through the silk and lace.

A small moan escapes my lips.

"Lady Victoria calls you slave. You are not yet worthy of being my slave. I shall refer to you as Pet. Moaning without permission and moving your lips are two more mistakes. You may tell me how many transgressions you have made so far."

"Four, Mistress." My crotch is moistening with every word she utters. If not for my panties, my wetness would be dripping down my thighs.

She leaves my shirt hanging open. She doesn't bother with unclasping my bra. Instead she pulls the lace cups down and lets my breasts pop free. My nipples are so tight and hard the exposure to the air borders on painful. She gives each of them a few tweaks before her nails graze the delicate underside of my breasts.

I gasp and shudder involuntarily. Being at her mercy with no light source is driving me past the brink.

She clicks her tongue near my ear. "That's two more infractions, Pet." Her tongue flicks out and licks the back of my ear, her mouth slowly lowering until she has sucked the lobe inside. I struggle not to squirm. Victory is within my grasp until she uses her teeth on me at the same time her hand snakes lower inside my skirt.

I moan again. The moment she called me Pet I felt a jolting tingle spread from my core to every extremity at once.

"One more," she whispers while running her finger inside the waistband of my underwear. She moves quickly. Her whole hand dives lower, cupping my mound. The sensations make me sway against her.

"And another," she murmurs. "You're so smooth and wet. It feels as though you want to be good, but you keep breaking the rules. Naughty Pet. How many now?"

"Eight, Mistress."

"It seems as though my new pet has a fondness for pain. Is that correct?" She spreads my folds until she finds my clit. Long fingers stroke my hard nub.

*How do I answer that one? I do not like pain. I like the rewards which sometimes come after.*

"Failure to answer. That's another. If you make me ask again you will reach double digits."

"No, Mistress. I do not enjoy pain."

She squeezes my clit until I moan again. "I think you lied to me, Pet. That's two more. What are we up to now?"

"Eleven, Mistress."

"Eleven?" she repeats with a note of disbelief. "That's more than one error per minute. By the end of the first hour you could be at sixty or more. Is that what you want?"

"Only if it pleases you, Mistress."

She laughs softly. Her laughter is warm and full of promise. She rubs my clit one last time before slowly dragging her fingers up, dipping briefly in my navel, then continuing upward, circling my breasts, past my collarbone, along my chin, and finally pressing at my lips. "Open."

I open quickly and begin to lick. She presses her fingers deeper and I suck them clean.

She withdraws them too soon and clicks her tongue again. "Such a bad pet. Did I give you permission to lick or suck?"

"No, Mistress. That's thirteen."

"Did you just give me your present tally without being asked?" The teasing breathy sound of her voice is gone in an instant. There is a sharpness to her tone now.

*Damn, damn, damn. How could I have been so stupid?* I keep mucking things up when all I want is to get something right for once. Instead I just make it worse.

"And now you choose to shut up so that I'm forced to ask my question again?"

"I'm sorry, Mistress."

"Eyes forward. The lights are about to come on. I need to see what belongs to me for this night. You, however, haven't earned the right to see me yet. If your eyes stray I shall double your count. What's your total now?"

The lights come on. I blink several times as I try to remember.

"Oh, Pet. You've forgotten, haven't you?"

"Fourteen, I think."

"That is incorrect. The number is fifteen. However, not following direct orders is a grave offense. Your number has just doubled to thirty. Now, stand up. Remove your clothes. Then, go and stand with your nose to the wall."

I hurry to comply with her instructions. The number thirty echoes in my brain. *Thirty what? Smacks with an open palm, a crop, a whip, a paddle, or...* I shudder and remove my last piece of clothing. I fold it and set it atop the small pile in the corner. I feel her eyes on me the entire time. She has a way of making me feel desired and just a tad uneasy.

I walk to the wall and don't stop until my nose is touching it. The sound of Lady M's heels striking the tile floor as she nears me is making me wetter.

"Arms straight out to the side."

I lift my arms and hold them in place.

"Legs spread. Shoulder width."

I do exactly as she commands.

"Mmmm," she expresses her contentment like a purring kitten as she presses herself to me from behind. She's still clothed. Her beautiful curves, covered in soft leather, slide against me. "Very nice, Pet. I see you can follow orders."

I swallow a lump of desire and will myself to remain still and quiet.

She mimics my pose from behind me. Her hands atop my hands and her body overlapping mine. The compulsion to turn my head and look at her is making me weak. Instead of turning I concentrate on what I can feel and smell. The tips of her fingers are warm. Vanilla and some exotic spice tease my nose. Something a bit rough slides over my arms as she begins to move. It's not her skin. It can't be.

Her fingers run the length of my arms. She alternates

feather light touches and grazes with what I imagine are long fingernails. She reaches my shoulders and her breath on the back of my neck sets off a trail of chill bumps.

There is a scar, roughly the size of a nickel on my left shoulder. The skin is raised and a light shade of pink. I feel the softness of her fingers circling the mark. I hope it isn't displeasing to my new mistress. I get my answer when I feel her moist lips bestow a kiss there.

"Are you ticklish, Pet?"

"Yes, Mistress."

"Is your safe word truly porcupine?"

I'm grateful to be facing away from her as a blush spreads over my face. "Yes, Mistress."

She chuckles softly. The sound is as inviting and as teasing as a lover's caress. "How on earth did you settle upon one of the least sexy words in the English language as your safe word?"

"An old lover. She introduced me to my submissive side. She liked them. Porcupines, I mean. I chose the word for her, and it just sort of… stuck. Pardon the pun." The explanation sounded far more elegant in my head, not rushed and jumbled. I'm too aware of who I'm speaking with, of what she's doing to me, of what may happen if she doesn't like my answer.

She laughs again. Her lips are close to my ear. "I think I might like you, Pet. I don't often get to see a guest's sense of humor in this room. I'm feeling generous. Maintain your composure for the duration of this inspection and I shall reward you."

"Thank you, Mistress," I murmur as her hands begin to move again. She alternates rough scrapes with her nails and teasing pinches and caresses with the soft tips of her warm fingers. She doesn't go in order either. One moment she's standing and touching my shoulders and back, the next she must be bent to tickle my ankles, then teasing the backs of my knees, under my breasts, over my calves, behind my neck, and back and forth until those skilled hands have traveled everywhere over my body. She even slides one finger deep inside me.

I'm panting. Other than my involuntary trembles I refuse to move. The urge to do something, anything, be it laugh, cry, fuck or be fucked, or at the very least move from her reach grows until it almost rivals my urge to come.

Just when I think I can't possibly take any more without reacting, she gives one last pinch to my inner thigh before her lips return to nibble my ear. "You did well, Pet. I now have a choice for you. You may turn around and look at me for a moment before we begin your punishment or I blindfold you and deduct five lashes from your tally."

Minutes ago I would have thought I'd have given anything to have my numbers decreased, but the thought of not being able to see this incredibly sexy woman, whose voice alone has me feeling like Niagara Falls is running between my legs, makes me suddenly blurt like Katniss. Rather than volunteering I say, "I need to see you."

I am rewarded with her soft laughter again. "Kneel."

I fall to my knees quickly. The chilly tile is welcoming to my overheated skin.

"Arms at your sides. Keep your eyes downcast as a good pet should and turn around to face me."

High-heeled patent leather boots with about a dozen shiny buckles greet my eyes. The heels are at least five inches high. The cuffs of the boots stop just below her knees. She has on sheer black stockings that hug her creamy thighs. I'm nearly overwhelmed by the need to bury my face between them. I breathe deeply through my nose. The rich scent of leather combined with the hint of her arousal have a dizzying effect on me.

The room is so quiet and my nerves are so wound up that when I swallow I can actually hear it. I wonder if she can too.

A gloved hand comes into view. The fingerless glove is

made of stretch lace. It was that which felt so rough against my skin. The glove appears long. It extends past her elegant wrist and travels upward somewhere I don't have permission to look at this moment. She skims her fingers along her inner thigh before grasping the elastic of her panties and sliding them to the side.

I am treated to a sneak peek of her smooth sex. No hairs, no razor bumps. It is the most perfect pussy I have ever glimpsed. My lips part and I lick them, wishing instead, I was licking her wet lips.

Her long legs take one step forward. Barely an inch separates her perfection from my mouth. I inhale another long, deep breath. I have but one wish. Her moistness glistens. She smells like raw desire.

"Don't you dare move." She speaks in a low growl before closing the distance and rubbing herself against my face. Another deep breath and I am lost in her musk. She begins to grind herself against me. I want so badly to taste her. Keeping still is becoming impossible. I keep my eyes and lips closed with a determination I didn't know I possessed.

\* \* \*

I'm not sure when I entered subspace. I only know that I must have because I don't remember moving from the room which only had a small couch for furniture. The next time I'm coherent I notice the air is cooler. The lighting is dimmer and at times seems to flicker. I am lying face down on what appears to be a massage table. There is a cut-out for my face so I am resting comfortably and able to breathe. My ankles and wrists are shackled. However my neck is not restrained. I raise my head.

Mistress sits before me. Her pictures from the ad did not do her justice at all. She lounges upon a throne with dozens of candles surrounding her. Her dark brown hair is pinned up. Smoky shadow and dark liner highlight her hypnotic eyes. Expertly applied candy apple lipstick colors her plump lips. I have not ever seen a more desirable woman in my life.

"I don't know where you went, Pet, but you were there for about fifteen minutes. I do hope you enjoyed yourself."

"Did you stay with me, Mistress?"

She nods.

"As long as I was with you then I am sure I enjoyed myself immensely."

The smile that spreads her lips hovers somewhere over the thin line of modest pleasure and sexy wickedness. "Flirting and flattery are fun, Pet, but they won't lessen your punishment. Do you remember your count?"

"Thirty, Mistress."

"Very good. Now, lower your head."

I obey her immediately, even going so far as to close my eyes.

Her heels tapping the floor are the only sound.

"Keep your head down. No sudden movements. I don't want to drip the wax anywhere it doesn't belong."

My eyes open wide. The pleasant temperature of the room suddenly feels ten degrees colder. A shudder races the length of my spine. My breaths are quick and shallow.

The first splash of candlewax lands between my shoulder blades. It's hardly painful at all, somewhere between a mosquito bite and a bee sting and yet I still find it nearly impossible to keep myself from trying to jump up off the table. The urge to scream is damn near overwhelming.

The second and third splashes land a bit closer to my neck and my willpower is just about completely gone. My eyes stay closed. Behind them, I'm somewhere else, back in Lady Victoria's Pit. The wax she used was too hot, too fast, had seemed to come from all over. I wasn't strapped down, not then. So I jerked up, trying to flee the heat, got the opposite result. The raw flame and a puddle of wax hit my left shoulder when she dropped the candle on me. I felt it for weeks afterward, but not as strongly as I feel it now.

"Pet?"

I struggle back to the present. I open my eyes. Lady Victoria is gone. In her place is the beautiful Lady M. The expression on Lady M's face is one of concern.

She has raised my head and turned it so I'm facing her. She's squatting beside me. Her eyes are just about level with mine. Tiny gold flecks swim in her chestnut brown irises. She no longer holds a candle. One hand soothes my neck while the other strokes my hair. "Are you all right?" she asks in that soft British accent that melts my insides.

A lump of emotion has formed in my throat. I try to answer but can't speak. I manage a nod.

She looks at her forearm and my eyes follow hers. Wax has melted on her arm. "I tested the wax on myself before we began. It didn't seem too hot." She stands up and begins to unfasten my bonds. "I do hate to break the scene, darling, but I must check that you're all right. I'm truly sorry if I burned you."

"You didn't burn me." I'm surprised at the hiccup in my voice. At some point I must have begun to cry. She uses the velvety pads of her thumbs to wipe the dampness from my cheeks. "Please don't stop. I need to be punished."

"You were on the verge of hyperventilating. Despite what I was told, it appears you have a strong aversion to fire. Why didn't you use your safe word?"

"The safe word is final. It brings everything to an end."

"It doesn't have to," she explains as she continues to unbuckle my restraints. "It can merely halt a particular act that you're uncomfortable with. The rest of the bondage games can resume immediately if both parties agree."

"I heard if I used the safe word then I would be told to leave and never come back. She said I could even be blacklisted as a sniveling wimp and no mistress would ever control me again."

Once I am completely free of my bonds, she pulls me to her, guiding my head to rest on her large bosom while she strokes my hair. "The mark on your back, that was a result of wax play gone wrong?"

I nod against her full chest.

"Is Lady Victoria aware of this incident?"

"She was the one with the candles."

Lady M stiffens in my arms. She takes a deep breath before pulling away from me. Her soft fingers nudge me under my chin until I look up and meet her steady gaze. "I may only have you for this night, but I need to make one thing very clear to you. Are you listening?"

There is a look of tenderness in her eyes. If it isn't genuine then she has skills that rival Meryl Streep's. "I'm listening."

"When you go home you are not to return to Lady Victoria. I will put you into contact with a respectable dominatrix in your area. One who knows there's a great deal more to being a Domme than bossing someone around and inflicting pain. She will look out for your well-being and ensure you are given both the pleasure and the pain you seek. You will also promise me here and now you will not be afraid to use your safe word if anyone ever pushes you too far. Understood?"

"Yes."

"Yes, what?"

"Yes, Mistress."

She smiles. "Very good, Pet, but that isn't what I meant this time. I want to know you've understood every word I just said to you. Repeat back to me your promises."

"Oh." I laugh nervously and apologize. I take a moment to replay the words spoken in her beautiful accent before I reply. "I promise I won't go back to Lady Victoria. I'll call whoever you recommend and if things get out of hand I'll say 'porcupine.'"

"Splendid." She rises to her full height. A coolness

settles over her. Her dark eyes narrow, full lips purse, and manicured nails tap on her sexy hips. "Enough distractions. I see before me a naughty pet in need of some stern lessons."

She crosses the room to a cabinet built into the wall. The sway of her perfect ass as she walks is mesmerizing. When she turns back to face me she's caressing a red and black leather flogger. "On your knees, Pet. Crawl to me."

I swallow hard. The strips of leather are wide. They look to be about a foot and a half long. *Thirty strokes from that and I won't be able to sit for a week.*

Lady M flicks her wrist and the tendrils crack in the air. "Don't keep me waiting." She cracks the whip once more.

I sink to my knees and crawl. My stomach is churning with equal parts want and fear. When I am at her side she orders me to stand and face the wall and I do so quickly.

A moment later her lips press against my ear. Her breath tickles me. "I've decided to give you fifteen kisses from this." She punctuates her sentence with another crack of the flogger. "And the last fifteen with my hand. You will remain still and quiet throughout. Understood?"

"Yes, Mistress."

"If you're a fan of police shows then I believe you'll know the position I want. Hands on the wall. Above your head. Legs spread. Bend slightly at the waist."

I hurry to obey. I'm expecting a hard lash from the flogger. Instead she runs its tendrils softly over my shoulders and back. It's warm and soothing. I bite my lip. Then lick it. A tangy sweetness greets my tongue. I swipe my tongue over my lip again as I try to place the flavor. I smile as I remember what it is. It is the heavenly taste of Lady M. She left a trace of herself when she rubbed her pussy against my face earlier.

I don't have long to savor the flavor. I hear the wind swish and then a blast of pain as she brings the flogger tips down across my back with quite a bit of force. Before I can brace myself, another blow lands. Then another. And another.

She varies her strokes. Some are hard enough to bring tears to my eyes. Others come fast with just a quick sting. One atop the other. Bam, bam, bam. I am sobbing now, struggling to remain on my feet and not cry out. The last few she spreads out until she has covered my back from neck to buttocks.

"Nearly finished, Pet," she says while hugging me from behind. The warmth of her leather-clad body is a comfort. "I want you to get back on your knees. Crawl to me at my throne. Drape yourself over my lap then beg me to finish your lesson."

I follow orders and watch her as I crawl. When she reaches her throne she turns around. She reaches her hands up and removes a pin from her hair. Her long locks fall past her shoulders as she gracefully turns her head from side to side. I didn't think I could possibly be more attracted to her and yet I am.

I am so wet. I feel the moisture collecting on my thighs as I continue crawling toward her. I am embarrassed to get up and bend across the stockings covering her shapely legs. I know she will feel the dampness.

If she does feel it through the silk of her stockings, she is kind enough not to comment. Her fingers glide over my throbbing back. The cool tips bring relief.

When I catch my breath I cough softly to clear my throat. "Please finish my lesson, Mistress."

"Mmmm." She makes that soft purring sound deep in her throat. "You're being such a good pet. I'm going to make you come so hard." Her hands drift lower until she's cupping my cheeks, then lower still until she's spreading my folds. "So hot and wet, already. Just imagine what will happen when I fuck you."

I sigh in delight and squirm against her knees. I am imagining all sorts of things.

Smack! Her palm lands on my left cheek. Then the

right, three times. Once more to the soft spot just above my crack. My eyes moisten again. Another smack to the left cheek. I lose count as my tears fall silently with every blow.

Almost as suddenly as the slaps began, they stop. She nudges me until I move back to a kneeling position in front of her knees. "You may thank me now, Pet."

I try to calm my breathing so I can speak, but she reaches her hand forward and places a finger on my lips. "Not with words, Pet. I have much better plans for that pretty mouth of yours."

My eyes meet hers, just for an instant. I see my own desperate need reflected back at me. I hear a soft moan, not sure if it's coming from her or me. I lean forward, my hands on her hips. I run my finger along the band of her panties. She braces her feet flat on the floor and raises her hips. Her intoxicating aroma makes my nostrils flare. I slide the panties off and fold them neatly before gazing upon her smooth sex.

I begin at her spread knees, placing soft, wet kisses in zigzagging trails from side to side and higher up until I near the apex of her thighs. Her breath has quickened. A small shudder makes her legs quiver. I revel as the tables are turned and I suddenly have some power over this beautiful, strong woman.

Her smooth pussy beckons me with its many shades of pink, rose, and coral. I map her with my lips and tongue, grasping her hips when she bucks. I know she wants me to go faster. As much as I also want that, I hold back. I do not want this delicious moment to ever end.

She is wet and open. I slide my tongue up and down her lips. Then, I dip lower and probe inside her. I piston my tongue in and out. After a while her fingers slide through my hair and she pulls me closer against her as she begins to grind against my mouth. A shudder rocks her whole body and her wetness more than doubles.

I keep licking and sucking gently even as more trembles

make her body shake. The second time she comes I hear a soft growl at the back of her throat.

I raise my head and she takes my hand. She brings it to her lips and kisses the back of it. "You were wonderful, Pet. There's a bed in the next room. Make yourself comfortable. I'll follow you shortly."

"But I don't want to leave your side."

"And I don't want you to see me hobbling like a newborn fawn, Pet. I need a moment to get my bearings. That tongue of yours is magical."

I smile at her, thrilled to know I pleased her. I practically glide to the other room. She wasn't kidding about a bed being in there. It's the only piece of furniture. It's much larger than a standard king and takes up most of the room. Royal blue sheets cover it. I step forward and crawl toward the middle. The coolness of the sheets feels so good against my battered back and ass when I lie down.

Thankfully Lady M doesn't keep me waiting long. I'm only beginning a fantasy of what her elegant hands will do to me when the door opens. She's removed her bustier, boots, and stockings. She poses before me in all her beautiful naked glory. "Do you like what you see, Pet?"

"Oh, God, yes."

"Good." She starts forward and gracefully settles on the bed. "Raise your knees and spread for me."

I quickly comply. I'm spellbound and dumbfounded when she brings her knee against my wet center. I expected her to plow ahead and get me off as quickly as possible the way Lady Victoria normally did. I should have known better. Nothing about the gorgeous and delightful Lady M is like Lady Victoria.

She leans in and settles her lips on mine, gently teasing and exploring with her lips and tongue while her knee lightly grazes my sex. The kiss lasts so long I am lost. I feel on the brink of coming just from this unexpected tenderness. I think I would have been happy just kissing her and sharing this incredible intimacy, but apparently it isn't enough for her.

She moves her mouth to my ear and gives a playful nibble that sends shivers racing up and down my back before she raises up until her nipple is at my lips. I'd wanted to suck it from the moment I first glimpsed her ample breasts in the leather bustier. Her sudden gasp lets me know she's as turned on by nipple play as I am.

I lavish kisses on both her breasts and rub my cheek against the valley between them while her soft hands skim across my skin from thighs to shoulders and every sensitive area in between.

She slides her body against mine until her mouth is back over mine. This kiss is even more intense than the last. Her fingers move over me, against me, in me. Then she's sliding again. Lower and lower. Stopping here and there to kiss and suck.

When she finally reaches my pussy with her mouth, I am long past teetering on the edge. I feel her thumbs spreading me slowly. Her soft tongue licks from my opening to my clit.

I push my hips up when her tongue leaves my clit.

"Be still, Pet." She pinches my ass. "Or I'll stop."

Once again I am reminded who is really in control. I lower my ass back to the sheets and enjoy her sweet kisses on my thighs and hips. She pauses with her mouth just above my clit. Her warm breath keeps me so amped up. "Do you want me to fuck you now?"

I moan and writhe against the bed. She remains still. I summon strength from somewhere and regain the power of speech. "Please, Mistress."

"Please what?"

"Fuck me."

I've barely uttered the last word when I feel her hot mouth take my whole clit inside and two of her long fingers thrust in me.

The pressure that has been building for weeks suddenly finds sweet release. I am unable to prevent myself from bucking and moaning as she continues to pump me even harder. I am sore and tender in the most enjoyable way as she keeps up with her gentle licking.

She coaxes me to one more orgasm then crawls back up to share in another soulful kiss. I lie in her arms and drift off thinking I may never want to leave Vegas.

# HIT THE TOP
## ROBIN WATERGROVE

The first time you hit the top, you know it. There's a point, beyond breathlessness and muscle fatigue, where your body will try anything to get you to stop. You're breathing so hard and fast that your lungs feel like they're caught in a perpetual gasp. The chest pains trying to pull your rib cage closed compete with the hot pressure of your heart trying to hammer its way out. Every muscle that's not burning with exertion is shaking because you have no energy to steady it. There's something thick and wet at the back of your throat.

You lift your hand to your face, and instead of rising in a straight line, it veers to the left and swings back in on its way up. Your fingers land imprecisely on your skin to wipe the sweat away, then fall back the way they came.

You can't get enough oxygen. At the anaerobic peak, your body does the impossible. It pushes harder still, with no air, no fuel for the machine, simply because you tell it to. In the thick of the chaos, you are in control. Stripped down to just your essence, your tendons. One side of your open mouth curls up into a snarl. You hit the top. The pain is nothing compared to the rush.

You're wiped clean. Reality's messy balancing act of intellect, emotion, and physicality falls away. You're all willpower. Everything else wilts in your grip.

It takes a certain kind of person to hit the top. You've probably seen us at the gym. I'm the one that's getting undressed with shaky hands, leaving my sweaty clothes in a pile under the bench, and walking to the shower with my eyes on the floor. I'm still coming down from an hour of cycling or lifting or swimming and I'm not ready to look at you yet. I feel too exposed.

Kind of like how I cover my face when I orgasm. Working out is a lot like sex. You get out of it what you put into it. Some of us are more committed than others to finding that high. Maybe we feel like we need to reassert control over our wayward minds and bodies. Maybe it just depends on what you like.

* * *

"Hi Joe."

"What's up, worker bee?"

"Nothing new." I set my lunch down on the break room table next to him.

"What'd you do today?"

He's asking what I did at the gym, like he does every day. We're creatures of habit. We do the same thing, over and over, all day long. Sit at computers, read things in one language, type them out in another language. It's a great job, actually. I can work whenever I want, as long as I get in 40 hours a week. For me, that means two to three hour lunches, most of which I spend in the gym.

"Spinning," I say.

Joe is eating a tuna sandwich, like usual. "Was she there?"

I nod through a mouth full of tofu. I wipe the back of my hand over my mouth and say, "Yeah. And super tan." My favorite trainer has been missing-in-action for the past week and a half. I had been talking circles with Joe every day at lunch, hoping she was on vacation, worrying she was gone for good.

"She looks good," I add. "She always looks good." Better than good. When I walked through the doorway into the indoor cycling room, I saw her crouching down, putting her shoes on. My stomach hit the floor and nearly pulled me down with it.

Just the sight of her sends me spiraling. It's less about

her body and more about how she carries herself. It's how strong she looks when her legs are bent and her head is lowered. It's the subtle swagger in her step when she walks. It's the way her head tips back when she laughs.

Joe is watching me. He says, "You should ask her out."

We've had this conversation a thousand times. The impossibility of the suggestion doesn't even trouble me any more. There's no way I'd actually do it. "What should I ask her out to do?"

"Some—" Joe waves his hand, "some kind of workout stuff!"

"I only work out at her gym."

"So start working out somewhere else and invite her."

"Is that even allowed? She works at a gym. Can she go to a different gym?"

He stares at me. "You are the most put together person I know. How can you not figure this out?"

\* \* \*

I work on top of the gym. Of her gym. My life fits together like a dollhouse city. I live in an apartment just three blocks from the office building where I work. At lunch, I come down to the gym on the first floor, work out, buy lunch from the deli across the street, and go back to my desk.

Some days I go by the Whole Foods a few blocks south; most days I forget. This evening, at home and grocery-less, I eat the heel of a loaf of bread with so much almond butter that my teeth stick together.

The real reason I've never asked her out is that she's never given me any indication she's interested. One time— exactly one time; I didn't need to try twice—I hit on her, pretty directly. I complimented her workout tights, she said thanks, and that they were hand-me-downs from Terri, another trainer at the gym. I said, "They look better on you," and she turned to me with wide eyes and said, "Wow." She laughed a little and I laughed a little and we both walked away. Then I avoided her for a week.

She's quiet, like me, so we barely talk to each other anyway. I wish I knew the secret to starting conversations because I'd love to know more about her. I wish I knew what motivated her, what she wanted.

I finish my untoasted toast and lick the last of the almond butter off my fingers. The floors in my apartment are always freezing cold in the winter so I'm wearing two pairs of socks and an old fleece jacket, holding my knees to my chest. Suddenly, loneliness takes a fistful of my insides and yanks down.

If I look my own motivations squarely in the eye, the curiosity is self-serving. I want to know what she wants so I can be that. All I want is to fuck her, be fucked by her. We never talk, so what is there to want but her body?

The first time I took a class with her, I was impressed by the silence. Most trainers can't shut up. But Jess—that's her name by the way—knows when to stay quiet. She cues us up for the end of a spinning track. "Thirty seconds left. Now push." Then she drops her head and rests her forearms on the handlebars, like she's making herself more aerodynamic. We ride out the thirty seconds with just the beat of the music coaxing us on.

I watch her face for the moment one side of her lip curls up. I like to be there with her, at the top. Three breaths from failure, legs burning, hands trembling. Suffering next to someone is almost like knowing them. Competition is a bond you can share with strangers, so even the lonely can feel like they've made a connection.

I guess I see the way intensity thrums under her skin and I wish I knew how to tame my own thirst for more, to be better, stronger, fiercer, and wear it so effortlessly. I see so much of myself in her that the extra parts, all the things she has that I don't—her confidence, her ease interacting with others, her commanding voice when she teaches—intimidate me. That's why I keep my distance. I would never sign up for personal training with her. The pathetically one-sided sexual tension would be too much for me to deal with. Besides, I push myself hard enough.

I cry on the kitchen floor for a little while. I don't ask myself why. Tears are like yawns. They just happen sometimes.

\* \* \*

It's January and the gym is full of New Year's Resolvers. My usual locker is taken, so I end up in an unfamiliar corner of the locker room. I'm in my bra and underwear before I notice her standing right next to me.

Jess is pulling on a bright blue pair of tights. She has on a yellow sports bra and a bunch of jewelry I haven't seen before. I startle, which startles her, and our eyes meet.

Now I have no choice but to say something. "Nice tights," is the first thing I come up with, which makes it seem like I'm watching her get dressed.

"Thanks. They've got weird seams."

"Oh yeah?" *Drop it, drop it, drop it*—too late now. "What do you mean?"

She finishes pulling the tights over her ass while I watch, try not to watch, watch anyway, then she twists to show me the back of her legs. The seams run from her inner thighs, down and back to the center of her calves, then around to the outside of her ankles. The line highlights her curves, the beautiful bow of her hamstrings. Trying for lighthearted, I say, "Weird in a good way, though."

"You think so?" Jess starts stripping the jewelry off and setting it inside her locker. "I've got thick legs and you've got to dress for your shape."

My head is racing, stumbling for something to say other than, *You're ripped. You have the most amazing legs.* What comes out is an incredulous, "Nooooo."

171

Jess just raises her eyebrows at me.

"Thick in a good way." The words are building, latching themselves to each other before I can think them through. "I'd kill for your legs. Like, you should be proud. Of them." I laugh nervously.

Jess is standing still, one hand resting in her locker. "I am proud of them." She's looking right at me, studying me. "You just have to dress for your shape."

"Oh yeah." Embarrassment becomes mortification. I'm nodding way too vigorously. "Yeah, I didn't mean, I mean that's good. You should be proud." Jess is already walking away from me, but I'm still talking. "That's awesome. Glad you are."

My chest caves in. I'm ready to avoid her forever but it's Tuesday and I haven't missed her Tuesday weights class in months. The only way to make this whole thing worse would be to call attention to it by skipping her class to work out alone. I get dressed with my face bright red and my heart pounding.

I walk into the studio, step around a set of weights on the floor, and hear, "Hey Sarah!"

When I look up, this girl I met last week, whose name might be Amy, is smiling at me. "Oh hey." I try to keep my voice down because Jess and someone I don't recognize are standing right behind her.

"Hey, do you run?"

"I, uh—" *I'm way too flustered to talk about this right now.* "Yeah, sometimes. I'm a little rusty." This is not true. I hate running with a bright and burning passion. It is the only cardio exercise that I avoid at all costs. But a lukewarm answer feels like a good way to end this conversation.

"When?" Jess chimes in from behind Amy.

"What's that?"

"When do you run?"

"Oh, whenever I can fit it in." Desperate to deflect the conversation, I ask, "You?"

"Five."

"In the morning?"

"Yeah," Jess says. The other women have walked away and it's just the two of us again.

"Well, I guess that makes sense. You always seem so busy, working here. I'm not surprised you get up super early."

"When do you get up?"

"Early. Pretty early." I nod with raised eyebrows. This is also not true.

"Wanna run?"

"What?"

"I do better with training partners. I need someone to run with. Do you live around here?"

My heart jumps into my throat. "Yeah."

"Meet me at Oak and 5th then. I'm off the rest of the week, so let's say Monday at 5."

"Okay, cool, yeah." Jess turns away and I say, "I'll be there."

After class, I race up to the office and fly in through the break room door to find Joe already at our table. His head snaps up and I pretend to faint.

He laughs, eyes bright and wide. "Tell me! What happened?"

"We have a date."

Joe's jaw drops and he jumps to his feet. "You what?" He rushes forward and grabs my arms, "You have a what?"

I shake my head with the ridiculousness of it, giggling and delirious, feeling like a teenager. I say, "We're going running. We're going to be running buddies!"

Joe's wide smile doesn't budge but he shakes his head slowly. "You hate running!" As though this is also good news.

I crack up and Joe hugs me. He hustles me around the room in a little jig. "Good job!"

\* \* \*

I'm so nervous Sunday night that I can't sleep for more than an hour at a time. I get up at 3 a.m. and put on my workout gear. I have a waking nightmare where I manage five steps at Jess's pace and then keel over with my hands on my knees and wheeze, "You keep going." I leave the house wearing brand new running shoes, which I hope she doesn't notice, and puffy insulated pants.

The reality of it doesn't really hit me until I'm at the corner of 5th and Oak, waiting for her. It's pitch black between the streetlights and there is no one but me outside in this frigid city. The sidewalks are slick with overnight ice and I'm shivering, breathing clouds.

Then Jess appears and my world narrows to the sight of her. She has on tights that show off her legs and a thick sweatshirt that rises in a fashionable cowl around her neck. It looks so soft. *What if we just hugged, instead of running?* I could say, saving us both the trouble, *I'll put my hands under your sweatshirt and keep you warm.* She smiles and I smile back.

"Ready?" Jess asks when she's close enough.

I figured we would discuss pace or distance or that she would at least give me a chance to warn her that I was going to disappoint her. But I just say, "Yeah," and she starts to run down the block.

Her pace is faster than mine at first. I don't know if I speed up or if she slows down, but we settle into a rhythm. It's an uncomfortably fast rhythm, but I can probably keep it up for half an hour. Jess doesn't talk and neither do I.

I focus on keeping my shoulders loose. What feels like half and hour comes and goes and we're still running. I'm fighting myself to keep my breathing in check, scrabbling to pull air in, then shoving it out again.

Fatigue is insistent, telling me over and over that this is too much. I reach the point where I feel like I absolutely have to stop, then push past it. I reach that point again, feeling dizzy this time, and push past it again. I reach it twice more before it feels like all the blood in my body is pounding through my neck and pooling in my legs, making them heavy and clumsy. I vow to reach the end of the block before I tell Jess I'm done, but once I've caved to the idea of stopping, I can't keep up the pace, and my steps start to slow. I see Jess start to slow ahead of me but can't find the energy to call out to her. I stop with my hands on my knees, breathing so hard I can't talk, can't move. Too much, that's much too much. My body keeps juddering like it's falling apart.

I don't hear Jess and figure she's run off until she says, "Good run." She claps my shoulder, sounding barely out of breath. I can't look at her. At least that's over. "See you tomorrow?" she asks.

I give her a thumbs up without raising my head.

* * *

Tuesday morning, my body hates me. I'm resigned to it, standing on Oak and 5th with stiff hamstrings, ready to run silently behind her for an hour. Jess shows up, smiles, and takes off.

This time I was smart enough to bring my phone. I wait as long as I can before checking the time. I count down the minutes until 6 am. It comes and goes; it's 6:06 and I'm still waiting for her to stop. Is she waiting for me to stop? I put my phone away and try to run like I'm not in agony, like I could run for as long as she wants to. I hit the mental wall, trip, find my rhythm again, hit the wall, over and over. I check the time. 6:17. My exhausted body starts to question my unwavering mind. *Why is this rewarding?* My knees are liquid. *What is the reward for doing this?*

*To be close to her,* my mind answers. *To show her I can keep up with her. That I'm worthy.*

I stop when I can't take it anymore. It's 6:31. Jess stops when I stop and claps my back. She doesn't say "See you tomorrow" and doesn't have to.

* * *

I show up Wednesday morning. My body accepts its fate. This is my life. Jess says, "Hey," as she walks up.

"Hey," my voice sounds different than it usually does around her. More settled, less nervous. Like something that has already been bent and straightened itself.

Jess takes off and I follow her. I didn't bother to bring my phone. When we're a few blocks in, she turns around and jogs backward. I jump, trying to rearrange my face from its miserable expression to something more neutral.

"Let's do some sprints!"

I stare back at her.

Jess turns around and yells, "Go!" She picks up her pace, driving her legs forward in huge strides. I try to accelerate and my body clunks and clamors. I'm stiff, my knees ache, my lungs are raw. I feel like I'm going to cry. Jess sprints to the end of the block and I run-trip stupidly behind her.

At the end of the block, we fall back to our normal pace. Two blocks later she yells, "Go!" and it takes me a moment to realize we're sprinting again. I run the block as fast as I can, feeling like a loose stack of bricks about to fall every time my foot strikes the ground.

Anger floods in, filling the cracks opened by exhaustion and confusion. *Hey, I'm doing my best.* Anger almost prompts me to yell it at her. We sprint again, then again. We're barely half an hour in but I'm at my limit. I can't feel my feet, my gasps are turning into wet coughs. I stop.

I hear Jess walk back to me and anger wants me to shove her. I see her hand come to rest, palm up, in the edge of my vision. I give her the weakest high five anyone has ever given another person. She says, "Nice job."

At lunch, I tell Joe I think I'm dying in stages.

"You're really plunging into this headfirst, huh?"

"I have no choice." .

"It doesn't have to be all or nothing though. Just tell her you need to slow down."

"What's the point of that?"

"So you can run without dying?" Joe looks incredulous.

"I'm not—" I'm too tired to explain. "I'm not doing it for my sake."

"Are you like," Joe narrows his eyes, "flirting or anything?

I shake my head.

"You're just suffering."

I nod.

\* \* \*

On Thursday it's sleeting. Jess shows up in a knit cap and I want to slide my fingers up inside it, stroke her hair, and kiss her. Instead, I run behind her. We do sprints again. Jess doesn't even announce them. She slows just enough for me to run up alongside her, then sways into me as she takes off. Each time, her arm brushes mine, or her shoulder knocks into me. I can smell her hair when she passes. It feels like she's taunting me. I run with frustration like a lump in my throat, feeling like I'm being used.

When we finish, or rather, when I stop running, Jess stops next to me and bends over. I pant at the ground and she says, "Hey, do you know any good sushi places around here?"

I swallow and steady myself just long enough to say, "No."

"Oh, okay. My sister is coming to town next weekend and she loves sushi. I'm trying to figure out where to take her."

I say nothing. I don't know if I'm angry at her or at myself, but it runs through me so thick and hot that I can't house any other emotion.

\* \* \*

Friday, I feel numb. When Jess shows up, I just turn and start running. We do sprints and I barely register the pain. I realize that before now, I didn't know I could push my body this hard. That knowledge is quiet and grim, not empowering.

When we're a few sprints in, Jess slows to a jog and says, "You sprint this one and wait for me at the end of the block."

I look at her, replay her words in my mind, and still don't understand. She shoos me with the flick of her hand so I turn and sprint. Unthinking and obedient. I sprint to the end of the block and wait for her. I stand, panting unevenly, and watch her jog up to me. She jogs by without a word, so I start running again.

We run a block and she slows again. "You go," she points to the block ahead, "Sprint and wait."

*What?* I stare at her and she stares back. *Now I'm working harder than she is?* What are we doing here? For the first time all week, my stomach twists, unsure, but I'm too weary to form a question.

I start to run. My feet pound too heavily, pulling my deadweight body forward. I sprint and somewhere along that block, I crack. When I slow down and look back to see her jogging behind me, frustration overflows. A rush of adrenaline sets my blood on fire and I start walking back toward her, my shoulders hunched and ready for a fight. I see her look up and begin to slow.

I meet her mid-block; the words come effortlessly. I spit, "What the fuck is this?"

Her eyes flick over my face and she says nothing.

"I mean, *what* the *fuck* is this? What are we doing?" I step into her, too close. My chest is shaking and my hands are throwing themselves wide in angry arcs. "Who do you think you are?" I'm right in her face, snarling now. Past my breaking point with no self-restraint. "What do you want from me?"

"Nothing." Her eyes flutter like she's startled. She shakes her head and speaks quietly, "But there's a couple things I'd love to give you."

My brain doesn't register her words. I laugh in her face. "Oh yeah?" I cock my head, a challenge. "Like what?" I feel like I'm going to throw up and I know everything I feel is spilling out of my eyes, contorting my face. Distantly, I know it doesn't make sense to get mad at her; I brought myself here.

"You know." Her eyes hold mine. "I've got something in mind with my tongue." She says it so plainly, like she's asking about sushi restaurants. There's sweat dripping down her temples. "My fingers, too."

And just like that, it's sex. It's like she's already inside me. Like I already gutted myself and invited her in to fill me up. She says it like it's been sex the whole time. My eyebrows lift. I stare at her and feel my stomach bloom with lust.

I have no quip to answer her and my anger is spent. I say nothing and kiss her instead. It feels like breaking. I'm breathing hard through my nose and when I open my mouth, her tongue finds mine. I whimper and she huffs. In a rush, my hands are in her hair and her arms are around my waist.

Her nose is cold and her mouth is hot. I feel like I've slipped out of my skin and into a warm bath. I press my hips flush to hers and she rolls against me in reply. Lust steers me, like it's holding me by the horns, and I kiss her how I want to fuck her. Dirty promises rise on my lips. I want to get her off on how badly I want her.

Instead I say, wetly, "You do this with a lot of girls you meet at the gym?"

She laughs. Her eyes are so dark and warm. "No."

"Why me?" It's more of a challenge than a question.

I've splintered and now I'm all sharp edges.

She speaks simply, not to arouse me or defend herself. "Because you want it."

Good enough. "You live around here?"

She nods, her mouth loose in an open grin. "Wanna come over?"

"Yeah."

Jess pulls away from me abruptly and sprints down the block. I watch her, feeling like a perfectly blank slate of confusion, for a few paces. Then she turns and yells, "Come on!" My swollen feet carry me after her. Running is a little easier when my body feels like a bundle of balloons on strings. Everything seems blunted and unreal. Even my own anxieties are dim lights under the vibrant strangeness of running back to her apartment.

I suck her neck in the elevator and murmur against her skin. Boundary-less and unashamed, I treat her like I know her, like I own her. She leads me to her door and locks it behind us. In another mind, I could have spent hours examining her apartment, picking through it for clues as to who she is. In this mind, I can't take my eyes off her.

Jess puts her keys on a hook by the door. "Kneel down," she says.

I hit the floor, knees first, with my arms limp at my sides. I'm still breathing hard. My racing heart accelerates arousal through my body, making everything tingly and light. I'm so wet it's making me wobbly.

"Take your clothes off," she says.

I stare up at her and unzip my jacket. I pull my shirt over my head and elbow my sports bra off the same way. I pull down my pants and underwear, all at once, with my thumbs. I collapse back onto my ass to tug them down past my knees, toe off my shoes, and shove the last of my clothes off my ankles.

Exhaustion makes me bold. I brace my arms on the floor behind me, lean back, and let my legs splay. Jess's mouth falls open and her hands twitch. She stands over me and takes me in with black eyes.

I've never felt more clearly that I was offering my body to someone. The thought of it makes my stomach flip. I put a hand between my legs and stroke two fingers up either side of my lips.

Jess lifts a hand to one side and says, "Get in the shower."

I do as I'm told. That's the point, isn't it? My legs are heavy and uncooperative as I walk to the bathroom. I run a hand along the wall and hear her right behind me. I have to hitch my knee up twice two get it over the tub edge. I turn on the water with shaking hands and lose my footing. Her arms fly out to catch me but she stops short. I let my tired body tumble slowly down, bumping my knee and stopping my fall with the soap dish, until I'm resting against the back of the tub, with my legs in the shower's spray. She hasn't touched me since we came back to her apartment.

"Is the water cold?" she asks in a voice I can barely hear over the static shower noise.

I shake my head.

"Make it cold," she says.

Here, frustration and anger and confusion invert themselves. I understand now. She has me where she wants me, where I want to be: naked in her tub, with broken resolve, ready to be taken. I want her to tell me what to do; she wants to see me do it.

My body responds to that realization with another shiver of arousal. I slouch and slip my way over to the faucet, not caring how I look, and turn the knob all the way to the right. The shower goes frigid. Icy water rains down and forces a reflexive inhale from my lungs. Inhaling against a cold shock is one of our deepest instincts. It's nearly unstoppable.

Jess knows this, I'm sure. She knows all about the body as it approaches failure. She's kneeling, bent forward with her chin resting on the lip of the tub. Her face is just inches from mine, watching so closely. "Is it cold now?" she whispers.

I nod.

Both of her hands are gripping the tub edge. She sucks her lower lip. "Does it feel good?"

*It feels like giving in to something stronger than I am*, I want to say. *It feels dangerous.*

Maybe she broke me so I wouldn't feel like I owed her anything, so I wouldn't mask myself. I let her have me as I am. I smile at her and open my mouth. I let the cold trickle in and fill me up.

Jess holds out a bottle of soap. "Wash yourself."

"Touch me," I say.

"Not yet," she says.

I take the soap from her and she says, "Make the water hot. To thaw you out."

I do as I'm told. Jess has me wash my hair with her shampoo, then she tells me to shut the water off. She hands me a towel and says, "You have a beautiful body."

I wrap the towel around myself and squeeze the water from my hair. My body is ecstatic now, on the long slide after burnout where it's happy just to be alive. Jess walks backward out of the bathroom and I follow her.

She takes me to her bedroom and gestures to the floor in front of her bed. "Sit down," she says.

So I do. Of course I do. I let the towel fall away and lay my body out for her at the foot of her bed. She kneels in front of me. The electric wait is too much. I moan and let my body writhe, getting off on her gaze. When I open my eyes, Jess is on her hands and knees, panting in front of me, searching my face.

Her eyebrows knit together. "You want to be touched?"

I nod.

"Then touch yourself." Jess says it like she's at the end

of her rope.

I laugh. Then I settle, because she's told me what she wants me to do. I stroke both hands firmly up my inner thighs and my mouth drops open. Her face mirrors mine, showing disbelief, hunger, impatience.

I stroke my clit with two fingers and tell her what it feels like with wordless sounds. Jess leans forward and braces herself around me. Her hands are on the bed behind my head and her body arcs around mine.

She still has her tights and sweatshirt on. Her hair is messy and her face is flushed. She breathes over me, her face pure desire and her body pure restraint. I know, in the way that things are obvious and indisputable during sex, that she wants me, so I make it hard for her. I let my eyes roll back in my head and get loud for her.

She closes her eyes and shakes her head like she can't take any more.

"When are you going to touch me?" I ask.

"When you tell me I can."

Our eyes lock. My sex-blurred brain rights itself and I wait for the murk to settle, so I can think clearly. Oh. Of course. I blink at her and put the pieces together. She may be the one driving us forward, but I have always been holding the reins. I say when the torture stops, when enough is enough. She stops when I stop. I nod to myself and she nods back.

I push her chest. "Sit back."

She rocks back on her heels and lets her hands rest loose in her lap. Then I finger myself until she's moaning with me and rubbing herself through her pants. For the first time, I make the choice to own the power she's given me.

"Tell me what you want to do to me," I say.

Her stomach contracts and her head knocks back. She makes a string of sounds I can't understand, then says, "I want to fuck you. Every way you want to be fucked. Till you beg me to stop. Till you come on my hand, in my mouth."

She's leaning in, getting closer and closer. "I want you to fuck me slowly," I say. She rushes to close the gap. Her head presses into mine, warm friction as she nods against me.

"Yeah, yes," she says, breathless and wrecked, "I want it. I want it, please." I see her hit the top. With her eyes closed and her mouth open, she's nothing but willpower.

"Take it," I say.

Jess falls against me, curls around me. She kisses me hard, with both hands on my face, then flutters them lower, flying to touch everything her eyes have crawled all over.

She rolls me on top of her and guides her thigh between my legs. My wet pussy marks the fabric of her tights. She pushes my body down and pulls her knee up, grinding into me. I feel two shaky hands caress my wet breasts, then drift back and grab my ass. She moans into my mouth and thrusts with her hips, moving both of our bodies in the instinctive rhythm of fucking. I feel taken, so I surrender what's left of me. I'm just loose strings and liquid sounds. I let her do what she wants.

Jess kisses my skin in long stripes from my collarbone down to my hips. She lays me out on her floor and goes down on me. She keeps coming up to blink at me with those wide eyes and asks how I like it, if I like what she's doing. I say it's good, really good, then I smile and push her head back down.

She fingers me so slowly that I'm mumbling, gasping, trying to tell her how amazing it feels when I squirt all over her carpet. It comes in waves, gushing out of me each time she pulls out her fingers.

Jess slurs, "Oh my god, again," with her lips against my clit. I take a deep breath and let her fingers take me right back to the edge. I squirt again as I orgasm. It wrings me out and radiates beyond my skin in rings of pleasure. I see her watching me, looking up through tangled hair, and I don't cover my face. She knows what it feels like to hit the top, so

I have nothing to hide.

# NOT YET
## HARPER BLISS

"Close your eyes," Ava says. "Trust me, you'll want to keep them open later. Give them a rest for now."

As if I can ever keep my eyes off her. But I do as I'm told, because this is Ava, and her command over me has incrementally increased in the time we've been together—and is now absolute. I can't say no to her pleading brown eyes and to that lopsided smile she puts on when she has things like this in mind.

I close my eyes and wait.

Nothing happens. But I've learned not to lose my patience. I don't peek through my eyelashes and try to figure out what she's up to. Like she asked me to earlier, I trust her.

She has me naked on the bed and a faint rush of air flows over my skin as she brushes past me. I've heard the sound of her rummaging through a drawer enough times with my eyes closed to successfully identify it. I also know what she keeps in that drawer.

"Give me your hands," she whispers in my ear.

I know better than to offer them to her in front of me. As part of our unspoken code, I bring them behind my back. She ties me up with something that feels like silk. It must be a ribbon of the red dress she made me tear up a few weeks ago. She'd come home looking ravishing in it, in full-on red carpet mode, still glowing from the attention she'd received. When I told her how good that dress looked on her, so good, in fact, that I wanted to tear it right off her, she instructed me to do so. And I did. The rip of the fabric in my ears, the touch of the silk in my hands while I exposed her glorious body to my gaze, was so intoxicating, she had me whimpering in minutes.

"That dress is a keeper then," she'd said jokingly afterwards, but she'd meant it.

I relish the memory of that night as she tightens the fabric around my wrists.

"Keep your eyes closed while you shuffle onto the bed. Make yourself comfortable." She follows up with a little chuckle because it's not exactly easy to make myself comfortable with my hands tied behind my back. Just standing up already makes me lose my balance a little, but, again, I've been in this position many times before. I take tiny steps backwards, turn around and, while bracing my core, bring one knee onto the bed. My other follows quickly and I only sway a little before finding my balance again.

"Better work on your core strength, Charlie," Ava said the first time she made me do this. I had toppled over face-first into the duvet, to Ava's great delight. Back then, she was still much more easily distracted and we'd both burst out into an uncontrollable fit of laughter. She untied me and allowed me to roam my hands all across her body while she fucked me. Not even if I fall over in the most comic fashion will she let me do that tonight.

The way she is with me now has been a gradual evolution of her pushing a tiny bit more every time we do this. The tone of her voice has changed from hesitant to incontestable. The touch of the paddle she sometimes spanks me with has grown from gentle grazing to determined smacking. Sometimes, in moments like these, when I clumsily shuffle onto the bed and try to find a position to sit in, overly aware of her eyes catching my smallest movement, I wonder where it will end. What she'll have me do a year from now.

I've tried fighting her for top, most times playfully but sometimes with such heartfelt passion it warranted a long discussion after, but in this combination of her and me together, this is how it is. And I've grown to enjoy balancing on that thin edge of curiosity, between wanting her to have her way with me in any which way she pleases, and the struggle that remains within me to resist. I'm by no means naturally submissive and we both know it—both get off on it.

"You can open your eyes now," Ava says.

I blink when I do and see nothing. I sigh, both with contentment and frustration.

"You'll figure out soon enough why I had to tie you up for this," she whispers in my ear from behind, then lets her teeth clamp down on my earlobe.

I've somehow managed to cross my legs underneath me and the touch of her teeth against my skin makes my clit pulse heavily.

Ava makes her way to the other side of the bed and I glue my gaze to her. She's still wearing the tank top and shorts she had on when she tied me up. I have no idea what her next move will be. She might delve back into the drawer, but she doesn't have me in the right position for a spanking. She might just leave me here to ponder her next action on my own for fifteen minutes, until my head is so full of possibilities—and my clit so engorged with lust—I'll be struggling to get my restraints off and put myself out of my horny misery.

Today, she does neither. Instead, she brings her hands to the bottom of her top and, slowly, pulls it over her head. I already knew she wasn't wearing a bra underneath, but the sight of her breasts being liberated, her nipples growing hard just by the feel of the air, unleashes another round of throbbing in my clit.

"It's really a courtesy to you that I've tied you up," Ava says. "You know what I'd have to do to you if you touched yourself of your own volition." There's that crooked grin again, accompanied by a wicked sparkle in her eyes. "I'm all about doing you favors, Charlie. That's how much I love you." With that, she hooks her thumbs underneath the waistband of her shorts and just stands there for a few seconds—mute and utterly delicious.

She's definitely doing me a favor by, ever so slowly, sliding her shorts over her hips and baring herself to me. As she bends over, her breasts fall forward and, by god, she was right to tie me up because if my hands had been free I would have grabbed for them in a split second. The combination of my impaired mobility and the sight she has me behold has me gasping for breath already. And I know her quick striptease is not where this will end, because that's not how she's wired. Not anymore. If I'm sure of one thing, it's that my hands will remain bound behind my back for a good while longer.

Amused and incredibly aroused, I watch her, waiting for what she'll do next. Even in the bedroom it's so clear that Ava was born to entertain—born for the bright glare of the limelight. She usually refuses to switch off the light when we make love, a decision I can always only wholeheartedly agree with because I'm at my happiest when I have my eyes on her, when the light—any light—catches in her glance and I can see how much pleasure she gets from sexually torturing me.

Ava now stands naked before me, her hands on her hips, a grin so triumphant on her lips it makes me fear the worst—or the best. I fully expect her to dig up that nasty flogger she bought a few months ago and have a go with it at my attention-starved nipples. Or maybe she'll go for the nipple clamps. She has that kind of look on her face that's not interested in mercy. Between my legs, I feel myself go wetter.

Instead of reaching for the drawer again and introducing another prop, she gingerly hops onto the bed and sits in front of me.

"How badly do you want to touch me right now?" Her face is a mask of mock-seriousness. As if she doesn't know the answer to that question already. As if it's not written all over my face that I want my wrists to be freed and my hands all over her magnificent body.

The only response that will preserve my dignity in this moment is complete silence. It's all part of the game. I purse my lips together, as though keeping them tightly shut will prevent any pleading words from spilling from them. I look into her eyes, trying to gauge her, the way I've done so many times before, but today, I truly have no idea what she has up her sleeve.

"Come on, Charlie," she spurs me on. "I'm not above letting you know that I really want to fuck you right now. Meet me in the middle here."

I remain silent, still fiercely braving her gaze. Though I'm getting distracted by the finger she brings an inch from my chin, by the promise of touch I know she won't deliver on. Not yet. She cleaves her finger through the air, the tip of it dangerously close to my nipple now, but our skins don't meet. Though for my nipple, she might as well just have pinched it hard the way it reaches upward, trying to catch her touch.

"Fine." She drops her hand and starts scooting backward. "But remember you asked for this. You know how I feel about these silences of yours." She pushes herself all the way to the other side of the bed, then clasps her arms around her knees chastely, her lips pressed together, as though giving great thought to something—like she didn't plan every single second of this before we entered the bedroom.

And there we sit. I on one side of the bed, hands tied; she on the other. My blood beats with anticipation. My clit feels like it might explode any second now.

Then, slowly, Ava lets her arms drop from around her knees and she spreads her legs, putting herself on full display for me. Instantly, my mouth goes dry. My heartbeat picks up speed. Because now I know how she's going to make me suffer. She's going to make me watch. We've done this over Skype a few times, but the big difference then was that my hands were not tied behind my back and I could take full advantage of the slew of stimulating images unfolding in front of me.

Her knees drop onto the bed and, her eyes pinned to mine, she inserts a finger into her mouth. She sucks it in deep, making a smacking sound when it leaves her lips. Then she drags it over her neck, in between her breasts, down her belly button, and holds it still in front of her sex. And it feels like she's doing this to me. In my tortured state, I can feel her wet finger drifting over my skin, halting a hair's breadth away from my clit.

Involuntarily, my wrists wriggle against their restraints. I want to break free. I want to do to myself what she's doing to herself. I want to mirror her actions and take the pleasure she's getting from them. But I'm not in charge of my own pleasure. Not tonight. Not yet.

She's not even moving her finger. It just lies there still. The only sound is the one I'm making trying to free myself and I know she must be getting off on the twitch of my muscles, just as I know that she has bound me tightly enough in order for me to not be able to set myself free. This pains me more than any smack she has ever delivered to my ass. The view in front of me is so sexy it hurts. My wrists ache from being bound, my shoulders from trying to wriggle free, but, most of all, my clit throbs so violently, I'm afraid I might climax just by sitting here. Just by exposure to air and the image of Ava spread open for me, about to touch herself. And that would be the worst sin of all. Not only because it would go against our unspoken rule that, in this particular situation, I am not allowed to come without her explicit permission, but, even more so, because for me, it would feel like a wasted orgasm. A quick shudder of relief that would not deliver on the anticipation that's being built up and up. I don't want a shudder from this, I want a dazzling thunderstorm.

I try to steady my breathing and, behind my back, clasp

my fingers together solemnly instead of fidgeting with the fabric around my wrists. I focus on my breath and, when I look into Ava's eyes again, I see she's waiting for me to calm down. To enjoy this in a way that doesn't ruin my eventual pleasure. Oh, how I will explode when she frees me and finally touches me. One flick of her finger and I will fall apart underneath it. But we're not there yet. I take another deep breath and try to tap into the stamina that I've built up being Ava's lover.

Then, her finger starts moving. She slides it over her nether lips, into the wetness that has gathered there. Her other hand joins the party and, with it, she spreads her lips wide, opening up her most intimate spot, for me. Though we're a world away from touching each other, we're so close in this moment. So wrapped up in each other. So completely devoted to each other.

Ava's no longer wise-cracking. Her mouth has drooped open. Playing with me the way she's been doing must have aroused her greatly and now, in the smallest way, it's my turn to enjoy her torture. Because she's actually touching herself and how can she not surrender to that? She will come under my gaze. My eyes on her will make her climax much faster than she'd want to. Inside of Ava's mind, a war is waging now. I can tell by the intensified motion of her finger around her clit. And, oh god, she brings a finger of her other hand inside herself and the groan that subsequently fills the room doesn't come from her side of the bed.

"Jesus," I moan. This is too much. The desire to touch my clit is so overwhelming I fear I might pass out. But then I would miss out on the spectacle she's giving me. One finger circles, while the other dips in and out of her, until she wants more and she adds another finger and delves them deep inside, as deep as they will go. I wish those were my fingers feeling the warmth inside of her, giving her this pleasure. I wish it was my tongue circling her clit. I wish so many things, until all my wishes are drowned out by the sight of Ava's stiffening limbs.

She's coming in front of me. Even though I'm not the one delivering her climax, the fact that she's giving herself up to me this way, showing her most vulnerable side as the orgasm claims her, I feel it power through me. The river my pussy has become will surely leave an irremovable stain on the sheets—a memento to remind us of this night forever. Her two fingers go deep inside of her as her muscles spasm, as her pussy contracts around her, and she furiously strokes her clit.

When she comes to, opens her eyes and finds my gaze, there's no sign of triumphant Ava. Her smile is soft, barely-there, her eyes narrowed in what looks to me like compassion. Because I had to witness this while imprisoned by her control over me.

This moment is a culmination of everything, because it's the instant before she will release me, but it's also the aftermath of her climax she had me watch, it's what this entire night has boiled down to. She knows it. I know it. It's why I don't mind her waiting a few seconds before she pushes herself up and gazes deep into my eyes, affirming our love, and this chemistry between us, and what our sex life has become as opposed to what it was when we first met. It's a recognition of the journey we've been on, inside and outside of the bedroom.

Then, finally, she comes for me.

She cups my jaw in her hands and kisses me as the smell that lingers on her fingers penetrates my nose.

"Untie me," I beg, when we break from the kiss, because I don't care about the game anymore. My skin sizzles with need. My clit aches with unmet desire. My entire body has become an extension of the want between my legs. I need her now.

Ava doesn't speak, just brings her hands behind my back and, as though she bound my hands together with the most uncomplicated knot, sets me free. My wrists are numb, but I don't take the time to shake some new life into them. Instead, I throw my arms around Ava's neck and pull her to me. Our breasts crash together, her skin on mine is hot.

I let myself fall backwards, pulling Ava on top of me. "Fuck me now," I say in between heavy breaths. "Please, fuck me now."

Not even Ava has the gall to not immediately honor my request. There's no more room for exerting control over me now. Time has run out. I'm sure, next time, she'll push me farther, but tonight, I've earned my climax.

She plants a flurry of kisses on my jaw, neck, nipples on her way down. I let my legs fall wide, allowing her to see the full extent of my arousal. I'm so wet I feel it trickle down my behind, coating my inner thighs. My clit is a pulsing heart of dire need, evidence of how her actions have aroused me. Wisely, she doesn't kiss it immediately. It would set me off straight away and she knows what I like when I come. One of her exquisitely long fingers inside of me at the very least. Or two or three. Wet as I am, three shouldn't be an issue at all.

I feel her breath move over me down there, feel her fingers skate up my thigh, along my lips, spreading my pussy wide. She plunges in two from the start, quickly adding a third, and I'm starting to lose it already. I'm in Ava heaven. Images of how she delved her fingers into her own pussy earlier pop up on the backs of my eyelids. Oh, those fingers and what they can do. They instantly connect with something deeper inside of me, with the need she has created by tying me up and making me watch her, by the desire that's been running in my veins since the day we met. Already, I'm starting to crumble under her touch. But my neglected clit is still thumping wildly, still waiting impatiently for the touch of her tongue.

When I don't feel her tongue touch down as expected, I open my eyes and see her glancing at my face, her lips trembling with focus, her dark eyes glimmering with love. I don't have to say anything because how could she not know. I love her and I want her tongue on my clit right now. I need release. I've been tortured enough.

Then, at last, she bows her head and, a split second later, her tongue is where I want it. Her fingers are still pumping, still bringing me to new heights, but the addition of her tongue, finally, lets me really break free. My hands are in her long, fanned-out hair. My pelvis is bucking up, trying to find some rhythm. My clit is melting under her tongue's caress. The sensation spreads through me. When my muscles start to shudder with orgasm, I relive the image of Ava sucking her own finger deep into her mouth. The same finger she's fucking me with now. It all blends together. What has come before and what's happening now. The touch of her tongue and her fingers. The smile with which she undressed earlier. The memory of the ribbon of red dress cutting into my wrists. And I erupt under her touch. My body gives itself to her completely, resulting in a loud, syncopated moan from my lips.

I'm free and I'm hers as she claims me with her fingers and her tongue, as the orgasm dances through me, reaching every extremity, saturating my blood, singing under my skin. When I come down from the cloud I was just on, the one that transported me out of my body and kept me firmly locked in its pleasure at the same time, I know that it would never have felt like this—this liberating, this earth-shattering, this all-consuming—if she hadn't played me so expertly from the very beginning.

With a contented sigh, I sink into the mattress, as Ava's fingers retreat. That victorious smile is back on her lips, but there's a subtle difference with the one she painted on earlier. A tenderness has crept into it. A tenderness that emanates from her entire body as she drapes it over mine and whispers in my ear, "I love you."

# LATIN LESSONS
## LISE MACTAGUE

Carmodie sat on the hard wooden chair and fidgeted, her thoughts turning wistfully to the sunshine outside. If she craned her neck, she could make out blue sky through the heavily-leaded panes of the room's small window. It was cracked open enough that the sweet smells of summer wafted to her on a gentle breeze. Distant laughter floated on the wind, mocking her confinement.

*It's not fair.* Her inner voice sounded petulant even to herself. *How* did *Father find a new tutor so quickly?* She'd only just run off the last one, a dried-out old stick of a man with a nasal voice and an unfortunate nervous tic that had only grown worse the longer he taught her. When he'd finally run screaming from the room, left eye twitching uncontrollably, she'd looked forward to at least a month of freedom.

It wasn't to be. There she was, barely a seven-day later, trapped in the same stuffy room waiting for the newest tutor. Even more alarming was her complete inability to winkle out the tiniest bit of information about this mysterious teacher. No one would tell her the least little thing about him, though her old nurse had smirked when she had professed her ignorance on the subject. Not even the palace maid-servants would fill her in.

She crossed the room and pushed the heavy window open far enough to look down. Laughter came readily to her ears. It seemed to be coming from the south lawns. Try as she might, Carmodie couldn't make out what was going on. Even on her tiptoes, she couldn't see over the small rise directly behind the palace. She gathered her skirts in both hands and contemplated the windowsill. It seemed wide enough and if she were on it, she could maybe see over the hill. Only the previous evening, the young women of the court had been talking about putting on a mock-joust.

Carmodie had attended plenty of jousts, and thought them a terrible bore. Men dressed like metal lobsters on horseback didn't really interest her. A mock-joust, where one boy sat piggy-back upon another as they ran about and tried to pull each other down sounded much more diverting. It would be diverting, watching the boys embarrass themselves for her amusement.

Her skirts were too wide to fit through the window opening, she decided and flounced over to the small desk. She threw herself down in the chair and crossed her arms over her chest. The tutor had two minutes to show up before she left the room, no matter what the guards posted outside had to say. *I really* am *a prisoner in here!*

Really, why did she even need lessons? She was eighteen after all, old enough to marry. Her evenings were filled with endless banquets as her father trotted suitor after suitor past her. She sighed and plucked at a piece of embroidery on her arm. The boys, with their prattle about hunting, were less than riveting. She expected they thought she'd be impressed. Not one of them ever thought to ask after her interests. The older men were even worse, staring after her with naked lust in their eyes. If one of them ever tried to touch her, she thought she might go mad. So far, no one had caught her eye and she was happy enough to leave it that way. Or she would have been if it hadn't been for these accursed lessons. As long as she was under her father's roof, the king saw fit to keep her days filled. There would be no idleness in the life of his only child.

The door slammed open behind her, the heavy wood thudding against the wall with a crash that sent her jumping out of her skin with an undignified squeak. A stern-faced woman in plain robes strode through the doorway.

With a groan she made no attempt to hide, Carmodie dropped her head to the desk. It hit the hard surface with a hollow thunk. *Not one of the Sisters of Perpetual Misery—Mercy*, she corrected quickly in her head, as if the woman could hear her. The holy women maintained a large shrine half a day's ride outside the city. The Sisters lived in a cloister just outside the shrine. It was the biggest Perpetual Mercy cloister in the Three Kingdoms, and it was known as the most humorless place in the realms.

"Problems, Princess Carmodie?" The sister's voice was just as dry and dour as Carmodie expected.

"Not at all." Carmodie didn't bother to raise her head. "What could possibly be a problem?"

An object hit the table next to her head. Carmodie jerked her head up off the table and stared at the nun in disbelief.

"Just what do you think you're doing?"

"That's one," the nun said calmly, leaning on the desk.

"One what?"

"And that's two." She watched Carmodie closely.

*Try it again*, a little voice in her head urged. It got her in trouble more often than not, but was so hard not to listen to. *Let's see what happens when we push it a little further.* The steadiness of the nun's gaze gave her pause, and she kept her mouth shut, though barely.

"So you can keep a civil tongue when you need to." The nun nodded to herself and her face relaxed a little. It wasn't enough to be called a smile, but she seemed a little less disapproving. "You may call me Sister Aulos. I will be tutoring you in a variety of subjects. Your father is quite eager to shape you into something he can use as a bargaining chip and I am to be the tool of that shaping."

Princess Carmodie sat straighter, heat rushing to her face. She knew her value, her place, but never had anyone stated it so boldly to her. It was always coated with platitudes and euphemisms. She opened her mouth.

Sister Aulos chuckled and Carmodie closed her mouth with a snap. The grin on the nun's face transformed her. She looked younger and less imposing and Carmodie froze, uncertain what to do next.

"Your father is a fool, child."

It wasn't possible for Carmodie to get any stiller. All she could do was gape at the woman smiling down at her.

A finger under her chin closed her slack jaw. The warmth of Aulos' finger was surprising and disturbing; something stirred deep within her belly. Carmodie snapped her head back and fixed the diminutive sister with a hard stare.

"I don't care who you are, you will not touch me."

The small smile playing around Sister Aulos' full lips disappeared as if it had never been. Carmodie shrank back before remembering that she was the one in charge. She stiffened her spine and stared defiantly at the nun.

"Quite to the contrary, Princess." A shiver went down Carmodie's spine at the steel in Aulos' voice.

"My father—"

"Your father is tired of your willful ways. I can certainly see why. He's given me complete leeway to see that you learn what you must. And Carmodie?"

"What?" Carmodie eyed the nun warily. Her tone had lightened much too quickly, she sounded almost gleeful.

"That was three, my dear child."

"Three what?"

Quick as a falcon in full stoop, Sister Aulos thrust her face at Carmodie who shrank away before she could stop herself.

"Your first two are free. You pay for the third one." Fingers like a steel vise encircled Carmodie's upper arm and she was dragged out of the chair.

The princess gasped in shock and surprised pain. Before she knew what was happening, she was standing by the nun, slightly bent over because of the difference in their heights. Carmodie tried to loosen the grip Sister Aulos had on her arm. The sister didn't even notice her struggles and the princess leaned even further forward when the nun sat in her chair.

"What are you—" A firm yank cut off her outraged words and Carmodie's eyes bugged out when she found herself lying across the nun's lap. She was still held captive by the hand on her arm and now Sister Aulos was pulling up her skirts with the other. "You can't do this! You can't! I won't—"

"You will," the nun said with quiet authority. "You will take the punishment that's coming to you. I won't let up until you apologize for defying me."

"Punishment?" It had been years since she'd been physically punished. The last time her father had spanked her, she'd been a little girl and he'd been so overcome with remorse that he'd promised never to do it again. "You can't punish me!"

"Your protestations are getting tiresome, girl."

With one final yank, Carmodie felt cold air on her behind. The nun had just pulled down her underwear, exposing her to the entire room. Her face burned in shame and embarrassment. A shockingly loud crack, and the cold of her rump was replaced with heat and pain. She cried out in shock. Carmodie clamped her lips together for the next stroke. The first smack had surprised her, nothing more. There was no way she was going to let the sadistic woman get the satisfaction of knowing she was hurting her.

A quiet laugh pulled her attention from the anticipation of the third stroke. Surprised, she realized the nun was smiling down at her. Was that approval she saw in Aulos' eyes? The third blow took her by surprise and she barely clenched her teeth on another outcry. Carmodie struggled, trying to get free, to get away from the pain scorching her buttocks. The nun merely shifted her grip and Carmodie could barely move. Throughout her struggles, the smacks to her behind continued until she felt like it was about to burst into flames. Sister Aulos showed no sign of stopping, not even when Carmodie could contain herself no further and hot tears spilled from her eyes.

Her struggles turned from escape to protection, but the nun just brushed her hand out of the way when she tried to intercept the relentless blows. It was never going to end; each loud crack brought a fresh wave of stinging pain and heat.

"I'm sorry, Sister!" The princess blubbered the apology through heaving sobs. She cried out when Aulos' hand rose again, and then snuffled in relief when the nun paused at the apex of her swing.

"You're sorry for what?"

"For defying you, Sister." Carmodie would say anything to stop the pain. This was so much worse than that final spanking she'd received from her father. "I'm so, so sorry."

The hand lowered and Carmodie buried her face in the nun's robes. There was never going to be an end to the pain, not ever. The nun would punish her until she couldn't take it anymore, she just knew it.

The blow never landed. Instead, the nun's hand gently stroked the abused flesh of her bottom. The gentle pressure soothed where it so recently brought pain and Carmodie relaxed, laying the side of her face against the scratchy robes. Gently the hand roamed over her behind, soothing the pain away, taking the heat with it.

No, it wasn't exactly taking the heat away. As her behind cooled under the nun's gentle touch, the heat was pooling at the juncture of her thighs where it grew with tingling intensity, spiraling outward. It felt... good. No, better than good, it felt fantastic. Carmodie moaned in startled response to the pleasure building within her. She pushed back against the nun's hand and was rewarded with a light smack. Sensation flared in her belly with such force that she bit her lip.

Experimentally, she pushed back again and was rewarded with another slap, this one harder. Carmodie buried her face in Aulos' robes again.

"Oh God!" she groaned against the nun's leg.

The nun let go of her arm and sat back. Carmodie lay frozen across her lap, afraid that moving would result in more punishment, and hoping that it might.

"You may sit up now, Carmodie."

Slowly, Carmodie pushed herself up and then stood. She reached back and pulled up her underwear, wincing when she touched her still-tender flesh and flushing at the jolt of excitement that lanced through her belly. She colored further when she caught the nun's too-knowing smile. Sister Aulos knew just how much she'd enjoyed that.

"I hope you're ready to learn now." The nun's smile widened. "We'll start with Latin today, I think."

Latin? Surely the nun was joking, Carmodie thought with a mental groan. It was easily her least favorite subject and no one except the kingdom's religious folk used the language anymore. Carmodie had no designs on a religious life, and didn't understand why it was so important she learn the language.

"Is there a problem, girl?" Sister Aulos watched Carmodie, that small smile playing about her lips.

"Not at all, Sister." Carmodie's response was hasty and her abused buttocks twinged, setting off an answering throb between her thighs. She lowered herself slowly into her desk chair, the same chair the nun had just vacated. It was warm and there was a lingering scent Carmodie couldn't quite recognize. It wasn't objectionable, but musky and it filled her with a longing she couldn't identify.

"Very good, Princess."

The nun's words pulled her back to the present. The approving emphasis on the first word filled Carmodie with pride at pleasing the nun and shame for being so eager to please.

"How much Latin do you know?"

"Not much, Sister," Carmodie admitted. "It's never

been my best subject. It's not like there's anywhere to practice it."

"Then we shall have to remedy that." The nun glided over to stand next to her. She turned a small book in her hands as she stood beside Carmodie. This close, the princess could smell the starch in the nun's habit. The scent was pleasant, and under it a slight earthiness lingered. The nun moved closer until Carmodie could feel the warmth from Aulos' body along her left shoulder and down her back.

The nun dropped the book in front of Carmodie. The princess shivered, goosebumps springing to life up and down the left side of her body from where Sister Aulos' breasts brushed against her shoulder blade.

"Pick it up," Aulos said softly, her lips not far from Carmodie's ear. The gentle shiver turned into intense arousal that tightened in the pit of her belly and refused to let go.

Her hands trembled and Carmodie willed them to be still as she picked up the book. It wasn't much bigger than her hand, but it was thick.

"Open it," the nun urged, her lips even closer.

"Yes, Sister." *Is that really my voice?* It was so hoarse, husky even.

The title page was difficult to make out, the scribe's handwriting was cramped and small. To her surprise, the title wasn't in Latin. *A Primer of Earthly Delights.* Carmodie licked her lips. It didn't sound like any teaching text she'd yet encountered.

"Turn the page."

Carmodie complied, handling the thick vellum of the pages with care. They'd seen much use and crackled when she turned them. The frontispiece seemed to jump off the page. The image should have been crude, the woodcut was simple compared to the etchings in her other books, or on the tapestries that lined the walls of her father's castle. She traced the edge of the illustration of two women, their limbs so intertwined she couldn't tell where one ended and the other began. One woman's hand seemed to have disappeared between the other woman's legs.

"Keep turning." The nun's voice was as husky as Carmodie's had been. Her lips brushed against the outer shell of the princess' ear and Carmodie was unable to contain her start at the long-anticipated contact. Warmth pooled anew between her thighs and the pressure in her abdomen increased.

All Carmodie could do was keep turning thick pages, helpless against the nun's urging and the fevered excitement their prolonged contact brought.

"Stop." Aulos flicked the tip of her tongue against Carmodie's earlobe.

She couldn't stop a moan and closed her eyes against the intensity of the sensation. Wetness mingled with the heat between her legs.

"What does that say?"

Carmodie opened her eyes and blinked, trying to focus on the word at the top of the page. "Cunni... lingus?" She stumbled over the unfamiliar word. It sounded Latin all right, perhaps she'd been mistaken about the book.

"Do you know what that means, Princess?"

Carmodie shook her head, not trusting herself to speak more than necessary.

"The word is in two parts. The second part 'lingus,' has its roots in which Latin word?"

"I don't know," Carmodie whispered. She gasped in surprise when teeth caught her sensitive earlobe and bit down, the pressure just on the wrong side of painful.

"That would be 'lingere,' or—"

"To lick?" Carmodie said, the term somehow leaping into her arousal-fogged brain.

"Very good." Sister Aulos' warm tongue soothed away her ear's lingering discomfort. Warm lips traveled down the column of her throat and stopped just shy of her exposed collarbone. Carmodie tilted her head, offering unobstructed access to her neck and realized the nun likely had a perfect view down her cleavage.

"I suppose a good girl like you has no idea what the first word 'cunni' derives from."

Carmodie shook her head, eyes closed and feeling only the wash of Aulos' breath warm upon her exposed skin.

"It's from 'cunnus,' Princess. It means vulva."

The word wasn't familiar to Carmodie either.

"It's the part of your body that's on fire right now, Princess." The nun's fingers trailed up and down Carmodie's upper arm. "Do you want me to show you?"

"Yes, Sister." The smoothness of Aulos' fingernails lingered against Carmodie's skin for a few more seconds. She exhaled in disappointment when she lost contact with the nun, then inhaled sharply when she felt the weight of Aulos' hand at her waist. She looked down and watched as the nun slowly moved her hand around Carmodie's waist to her belly. The pressure in her abdomen increased, building to a fever pitch and she whimpered at the relentless pleasure.

"Look at me," Sister Aulos commanded and when Carmodie glanced up, her eyes were caught and held by the nun's. She saw as much desire staring back at her as she felt, though Aulos' was tempered just a bit by amusement.

The nun leaned closer until her breath was warm upon Carmodie's lips. The warmth that had been growing between her thighs flared to an inferno of need and she looked down. The nun's hand was over her crotch, the fingers curling down around her mound and cupping her through the gown's many layers of fabric. Carmodie's breathing hitched at seeing the nun's hand on her most private of parts.

"Princess." Aulos' voice held a stern warning and Carmodie looked back into her eyes. The nun leaned forward and covered Carmodie's lips with her own. Aulos' lips moved against hers, fanning her arousal still further until Carmodie dazedly wondered why she didn't burst into flames.

When Sister Aulos tightened her hand on her center, Carmodie gasped and the nun slipped her tongue inside the princess' mouth. Awash in a sea of sensation, Carmodie wrapped both arms around Aulos and held on for dear life. She was aware of nothing, save for the tongue that savored and teased her mouth, and the hand that moved over her mound, rubbing her through layers of fabric until she was no more than an aching ball of need.

Some time later, the nun lifted her head and they stared at each other, chests heaving.

"I want you to pay close attention, Princess," Aulos said, her voice raspy. "This is the most important part of today's lesson and you will be tested."

She watched dumbly as the nun knelt in front of her.

"Sister!" Her shock came out in her voice when she felt warm hands around her ankles.

"Do you want me to stop, Carmodie?" There was no trace of amusement on Aulos' face now. "I can stop now or I can give you pleasure greater than any you have felt before in your life. It's your decision."

Aulos was still and she crouched, as if awaiting Carmodie's response. She made no attempt to change the princess' mind with wheedling or flattery. Instead, she put the decision in Carmodie's hands, trusting that the princess had all the information she needed to decide for herself.

Though she was a princess, Carmodie rarely made her own decisions. Even those decisions that were ostensibly hers, others tried to influence, through bribery or in carefully veiled threats.

In that moment, and despite her still-aching behind—or perhaps because of it—Carmodie decided she could trust the nun.

"Very—" Her throat was dry and she had to swallow hard. "Very well."

The nun's eyes flashed, betraying a need as deep as her

own, and Aulos smiled. "What is it you want?"

"I want to learn my lesson, Sister."

The hands that had been so warm around her ankles traveled upward, warming her calves, her knees, her thighs. Warmth was replaced by chill air as her legs were exposed to the coolness of the room.

Carmodie moaned in disappointment when the nun reached her bloomers and she lost the delicious feeling of skin against hers.

"Patience, Princess." Aulos' voice held a wicked edge. "It's a virtue."

"There's no virtue in what you're doing."

The nun's laugh was startled but genuine.

Carmodie felt a pang of relief, followed quickly by disappointment that she wasn't going to be punished again.

With a quick tug, Aulos pulled down Carmodie's voluminous drawers. The room's slightly chilled air washed over the hot and moist flesh of her sex. Instead of soothing, it only enflamed her passions further.

"Sister..." This time she entreated instead of ordering.

Cool air warmed, replaced by hot breath that caressed her. Unable to stop herself, Carmodie cried out. Moisture trickled down her slit in time to be captured by the tip of Aulos' tongue.

Her hips gave a convulsive jerk and the nun shifted, not letting up on the gentle pressure she exerted on the inside of Carmodie's vulva. The nun wrapped her arms around Carmodie's legs and anchored her in place, a fact the princess was only dimly aware of. Her hips continued to twitch with every pass of Aulos' tongue. With desperate hands, she grabbed the sides of the chair's seat, holding on for dear life. She had the sense that she was building toward something glorious. Pressure increased in her abdomen and overflowed between her thighs. Liquid literally dripped from her and the nun's eager tongue lapped it up as quickly as it was produced.

When the movement of the tongue between her legs ceased, Carmodie slowly realized she had her eyes clenched shut and her head was thrown back. She whipped her head around and opened her eyes just in time to meet Sister Aulos' wicked gaze. The nun grinned up at her, the tip of her tongue visible between her teeth and lower lip. Satisfied that she had the princess' full attention, Aulos smiled wider. Her eyes danced and she leaned forward, not breaking their locked gazes.

In one swift movement, the nun's tongue stopped teasing and entered her, probing Carmodie's most intimate place. It withdrew and entered her again. Then again. And again.

The pleasure that had been building to such a fever pitch crested and thundered through her. Light crawled behind her eyelids and her hips heaved against the nun's mouth. The scream that issued from Carmodie's lips overflowed with passion and utter abandon. If she hadn't felt it as it was torn from her, Carmodie would never have believed that the voice was hers.

She rode wave after wave of pleasure before coming back to herself in pieces. Harsh panting filled her ears and she tried to slow her breathing. The tightening of the hands around her legs demanded her attention. Carmodie looked down at Aulos again. Her thighs were clamped around the nun's head, holding her immobile.

"I'm so sorry, Sister!" Hurriedly, Carmodie spread her legs.

"In the future, Princess, when I tap on your thighs, I expect them to open." The nun's expression was grave as she straightened. Moisture glistened on the lower half of her face. Carmodie watched, fascinated, as the nun licked her lips. "Is that clear, Princess?" Aulos punctuated the question with a stinging slap to her thigh.

"Y-yes, Sister Aulos."

"Good." The nun soothed the slightly tingling flesh of

Carmodie's thigh with soft caresses. "I'll let it slide this time, but do not test me again."

"No, Sister."

The nun smiled and Carmodie couldn't help but smile back. "You show excellent aptitude, Highness."

"Thank you." Carmodie paused before continuing. "I hope there will be more lessons."

"This is the first of many lessons, you may be assured of that. By the time you've completed my tutelage, you will be proficient—nay expert—in numerous areas."

Carmodie smiled. "I can't wait."

"I know, Princess. And you'll test me." She raised a finger when Carmodie opened her mouth to protest. "You will. It's in your nature. Never fear, when you test me, I will punish you accordingly."

Carmodie shivered, the space between her thighs already growing wet in anticipation. Sister Aulos noticed the shudder and smirked knowingly. Her hooded eyes promised great pain and even greater pleasure and Carmodie felt the smile on her face widening to match the nun's.

"Now, Princess," Sister Aulos said. "It's time for your first exam. I hope you were paying close attention."

"Sister?" Carmodie licked her lips. She wasn't sure if she was nervous or excited. From the way butterflies swirled madly in her stomach and lower, it was more than a bit of both.

"As delectable as you are, my dear, surely you didn't think you would be the only one brought to satisfaction?"

"Yes, Sister." When Aulos' face darkened, Carmodie waited a moment before amending her statement. "I mean, no, Sister."

"Very well." From the small smile that played around the nun's lips, she hadn't missed Carmodie's pause.

Was she really trying for another spanking? Her belly clenched at the thought.

The nun watched Carmodie, waiting, daring her to dally

again. She decided not to push it too far, though a dark place deep within her urged her to nudge the nun just a little further. The floor was cold against her knees. Carmodie warmed at the approval in the nun's eyes. Relief and disappointment flooded through her.

Never breaking eye contact, Sister Aulos settled herself in the chair. She stared at Carmodie but said nothing. With a start, Carmodie realized the nun was waiting for her to begin.

She tentatively reached out a hand toward the stiff skirts of Aulos' habit. The clearing of the nun's throat pulled her attention upward.

"You will request permission before you touch me, Princess."

"But you didn't have to."

A sudden vise gripped her wrist and Carmodie gasped. She hadn't even seen the nun move, but Sister Aulos' hand clamped down on her. She could feel the nun's breath on the side of her cheek when Aulos leaned forward to speak.

"Do not forget who is the teacher, and who is the pupil."

"Yes, Sister Aulos." Carmodie squeaked when Aulos released her as quickly as she'd been grabbed.

"Good. Now go on."

"May I touch you, Sister Aulos?" Her voice wavered slightly and Carmodie cleared her throat.

"Why do you wish to touch me, my dear Princess?"

"To bring you pleasure, Sister Aulos."

"And how do you plan to do that, Carmodie?"

"Cunnilingus." Carmodie barely stumbled over the still unfamiliar word. Pride warmed her at the nun's approving smile.

"Very well. You may touch me."

Slowly, Carmodie reached forward again. When there was no sign of displeasure from Aulos, Carmodie trailed her fingers down the scratchy black fabric. She could hardly feel the nun's legs beneath the stiff material. Carmodie wondered how many layers of skirts there were.

Her fingers trembled slightly in anticipation while her center was awash with heat. Would Sister Aulos feel as hot as she did?

The top layer of skirts proved to be little more than an apron, and she moved it aside easily enough. The skirts below were heavier. She was quickly flustered by the voluminous underskirts and she blushed, suddenly embarrassed by how awkward she must seem.

"Take your time, Princess."

The murmured instruction did little to make Carmodie feel better, but she was learning better than to disobey orders. With a deep breath and deliberate pace, Carmodie attacked her task.

The dark skirts were finally out of the way and Carmodie gaped at the nun's bare legs. They were pale, almost luminous and with no flaws that she could see. As she stared, Aulos shifted and spread her thighs. To Carmodie's shock, the nun wore no underclothes, not even the smallest of bloomers. She couldn't see all the way up, and Carmodie's curiosity and powerful arousal drove her on.

She placed her hand on one of Aulos' knees and smiled at the quiet moan she drew from the nun's throat. Knowing she had the power to elicit such a reaction from the obviously more experienced nun gave Carmodie a boost of confidence. She slid both her hands slowly upward.

The nun's skin rivaled even the smoothest silk. The warmth of her skin pulled Carmodie on, desperate to feel even more of Aulos beneath her fingers. The nun's skirts crept ever higher, exposing more of her legs to the somewhat chill air.

Finally, the skirts no longer obscured Carmodie's view of her target. Even from where she knelt on the cold stone floor, Carmodie could see that Aulos was wet. She was aware of answering wetness between her own thighs. It was more than dampness, she was drenched with excitement, and Aulos clearly wasn't very far behind.

The delicious-looking folds of coral skin at the apex of the nun's thighs begged for her touch. Carmodie lightly traced the outside of Sister Aulos' lips. Her fingertips tangled gently through springy hair which she moved out of the way for an even better look.

The nun's vulva was more complex than she had imagined. The outer folds masked a delicate inner structure of even more folds topped by a small nub. If she wasn't mistaken, that was one of the places that had given her so much pleasure. She brushed lightly against the folds with a gentle fingertip. Aulos' entire body twitched in convulsive reaction. Carmodie felt her own center echo the nun's response.

If the mere touch of her finger was that successful, surely her tongue would please the nun even further. Carmodie leaned forward, inhaling deeply as she moved. The scent of Aulos' excited sex washed over her, pulling a moan from deep within her own throat. The nun smelled musky and ripe with promise; Carmodie's mouth watered in anticipation.

Unable to wait any longer, Carmodie buried her face in the damp heat between the nun's thighs. With her questing tongue, she parted the folds around Aulos' entrance.

Fingers entwined in her hair, holding her in place. Emboldened by the mute encouragement, Carmodie thrust her tongue into the nun. She was rewarded by a sharp intake of breath and the tightening of the fingers in her hair. The tugs on her hair sent sensation coursing from the roots to her center and she moaned into the nun's heat.

"My God, Princess." Aulos could barely choke out the words; her voice was thick with desire.

Carmodie thrust into the nun again. Aulos shifted her hips to meet her, using the grip she had on Carmodie's head to keep the princess in place.

Her hips rose and fell faster now as Carmodie redoubled her efforts. She slid the tip of her tongue from Aulos' opening and up the slick strip of skin until she reached the tantalizing nub of flesh at the top of the nun's folds. This was what had felt so good when Aulos had her lips on her. Carmodie's sex throbbed in response when she reached Aulos' nub.

The nun's hoarse cry was all the encouragement she needed. Carmodie licked the length of her folds again, ending with the little bundle at the top and was rewarded with another cry and the convulsive twitch of the nun's entire lower half.

Harsh panting filled the air and wetness smeared the lower half of Carmodie's face. The nun seemed to be past all coherent thought. She thrust her hips in time with the swipe of Carmodie's tongue. There was no sense to the words that spilled from her lips. Aulos babbled an irreverent stream of nonsense that Carmodie would have been shocked to hear had she not been crouched with her head buried between the nun's legs.

She panted out her own excitement. The closer Aulos got to that pinnacle of pleasure to which she'd so recently introduced the princess, the more excited Carmodie became in her own right.

She moved her hand from where she gripped the nun's thigh. Aulos didn't seem to notice the change, but she did notice when Carmodie stopped licking. Her hands gripped Carmodie's hair. The pressure was just the right side of painful. Carmodie moaned and closed her eyes.

"What are you doing, Princess?" Aulos glared down at her, chest heaving.

"I want to feel you," Carmodie said. She took one finger and slowly pressed it inside the nun.

Aulos gasped and swayed like a tree in a high wind. "Clever girl."

Carmodie grinned, pleased by the strength of Aulos'

reaction. What she felt around her finger made her bite her lip. The nun's damp walls pulled her deeper and she slid all the way in, until she could go no further.

"Another one." Aulos' voice shook.

Carmodie pushed in with another finger. Aulos shifted forward to meet her thrust. Her eyes were closed and her head was thrown back. She seemed blind and deaf to everything except what Carmodie was doing to her. If a troop of palace guards had wandered in and started performing parade ground maneuvers, Aulos would likely never have known. A thrill shot through Carmodie at the realization that she was the one providing so much pleasure to the nun.

Aulos rode her fingers. One hand still tangled in Carmodie's hair, the other gripped her shoulder. The nun's eyes were squeezed shut and she breathed heavily through gritted teeth. Aulos seemed to be chasing something just out of reach. Those damp walls rippled around Carmodie's pumping digits, slowly at first, then faster.

Suddenly, the nun stiffened, her back arching as she impaled herself fully on Carmodie's fingers. Her mouth opened in a silent shout and her grip tightened for long moments. Finally, Aulos relaxed, and let her hand drop to Carmodie's other shoulder.

Delighted, Carmodie watched an expression of peace settle over the nun's face. She had done all that with only her tongue and two fingers.

"Well done, Princess." Aulos smiled tiredly down at her. "You have passed your first exam with the highest marks."

"Thank you, Sister Aulos." Carmodie pulled her fingers slowly from the nun's opening. "I have enjoyed my lesson." Juices coated her fingers and she stuck them in her mouth to clean them, savoring the sweet deliciousness.

"I thought you might," Aulos said fondly. She stretched expansively before drawing one finger down the side of

Carmodie's cheek. "And if you enjoyed that, the lessons to come will be even more to your liking."

# ABOUT THE EDITOR

Harper Bliss is the author of the novels *Seasons of Love*, *Release the Stars*, *Once in a Lifetime* and *At the Water's Edge*, the *High Rise* series, the *French Kissing* serial and several other lesbian erotica and romance titles. She is the co-founder of Ladylit Publishing, an independent press focusing on lesbian fiction. Harper lives on an outlying island in Hong Kong with her wife and, regrettably, zero pets.

Harper loves hearing from readers and if you'd like to drop her a note you can do so via harperbliss@gmail.com

Website: www.harperbliss.com
Facebook: facebook.com/HarperBliss
YouTube: youtube.com/c/HarperBliss

# ABOUT THE CONTRIBUTORS

EDEN DARRY lives in London with her partner and their small, earless rescue cat. She runs her own business, and when she's not working or writing, can usually be found rowing up and down the Thames.

LUCY FELTHOUSE is the award-winning author of erotic romance novels *Stately Pleasures* (named in the top 5 of Cliterati.co.uk's 100 Modern Erotic Classics That You've Never Heard Of, and an Amazon bestseller) and *Eyes Wide Open* (an Amazon bestseller). Including novels, short stories and novellas, she has over 140 publications to her name. She owns Erotica For All, is book editor for Cliterati, and is one eighth of The Brit Babes. Find out more about her writing at http://lucyfelthouse.co.uk, or on Twitter and Facebook.

S.E. HILL lives in Florida. Krista, the pretty girl that inspires every dirty word she writes, lives in Tennessee. Yet, the distance doesn't seem to stop either from living out their fantasies with one another. Krista pops up as a character in most of S.E. Hill's stories. S.E. Hill would also like to give special thanks to T. Henry, whose exceptionally dirty mind planted the seed for this particular story.

ELNA HOLST is a translingual, crossgeneric storyteller, born outside Malmö, Sweden. Most of her adult life has been spent going back and forth between this country and Scotland, where she worked, wrote and studied through her 20's. Since 2009, she is back in the old country, supporting herself through the many and varied pursuits of her pen and keyboard.

LAUREN JADE grew up on a farm in rural Tennessee, but moved to the city seeking romance, adventure, and an education. She is a freelance writer who lives near Nashville with her partner and their two-legged and four-legged sons. She holds a Bachelor of Music, and teaches and performs throughout the greater Nashville area. Lauren is a marathon runner, wine lover, nature enthusiast, and coffee addict. Her first short story, *Kissing Whiskey*, was published as part of *Appetites, Tales of Lesbian Lust*.

J. BELLE LAMB holds an M.F.A. in poetry. She's taught writing at the university and high school levels. Currently she lives on an island in the Pacific Northwest, where she wishes she'd run into more hot butches. She's active in her local kink scene.

SAMANTHA LUCE lives in the Mosquito state a.k.a. Florida. She works in law enforcement. In her spare time, she writes fan fiction, reads whatever she can get her hands on, and is currently at work on a lesbian thriller featuring a kick-ass FDLE agent and a sexy deputy sheriff. She has one other short story published in *Don't Be Shy*, edited by Astrid Ohletz and Jae.

LISE MACTAGUE is the author of *Depths of Blue* and *Heights of Green*, and is a hockey player, and librarian. Her parents had their priorities straight and introduced her to sci-fi at the age of three through reruns of Star Trek, and she's been living in the speculative fiction universe ever since. Lise lives in Milwaukee with her girlfriend and their four cats.

ROBYN NYX is an avid shutter-bug and lover of all things fast and physical. Her writing often reflects both of those passions. She writes lesbian fiction for Bold Strokes Books when she isn't busy being the Chief Executive of a UK charity. She lives with her soul mate and fellow filth peddler — they have no cats or children, which allows them to travel to exotic places at the drop of a hat for 'research.' She tries hard to write daily, but can sometimes be distracted by blue skies and motorbike rides.

JANELLE RESTON (janellereston.tumblr.com) lives in the Upper Midwest with her partner and three cats. She has also published lesbian femdom fiction in *To Obey Her*.

SINCLAIR SEXSMITH is a genderqueer kinky butch writer who teaches and performs, specializing in sexualities, genders, and relationships. They've written at sugarbutch.net since 2006, recognized numerous places as one of the Top Sex Blogs. Sinclair's gender theory and queer erotica is widely published in anthologies and online, and they are the editor of *Best Lesbian Erotica 2012* and *Say Please: Lesbian BDSM Erotica*. *Sweet & Rough: Sixteen Stories of Queer Smut*, Sinclair's first collection of short stories, was published in 2014. They use the pronouns they, them, theirs, themself.

LEANDRA VANE writes a book review and sexuality blog entitled *The Unlaced Librarian*. Her work tackles concepts in body identity, disability, and kink. She drinks too much tea and changes the names of her lipstick shades to suit her muse.

ROBIN WATERGROVE writes at a messy desk in a neat room. She loves sunshine, goofy jokes, and coffee popsicles. She writes to capture life as it is, believing empathy to be a better medicine than escape, and considers the highest praise to be 'I've felt that, too.' Robin lives in the Pacific Northwest and tells everyone that it's rainy and grey so she can have the lovely weather all to herself. She doesn't have any pets but there is this one neighborhood cat that badly wants to live in her house. They hang out on her porch instead.

BROOKE WINTERS lives in the UK. Her first short story, Mistress, was published in Ladylit's Summer Love anthology. Brooke blogs at brookewinters.wordpress.com and you can find her on Twitter.

Printed in Great Britain
by Amazon